CAPTURED

CAPTURED

MICHAEL SERRIAN

A Critic's Choice paperback
from Lorevan Publishing, Inc.
New York, New York

ISBN: 1-55547-117-3

First Critic's Choice edition: 1987

From LOREVAN PUBLISHING, INC.

Critic's Choice Paperbacks
31 E. 28th St.
New York, New York 10016

Manufactured in the United States of America

Acknowledgments

Thanks to Len Leone for his extraordinary cover concept and design. To Jerry Koril for his "creative" input. The technical expertise of Curtis Manley and the gang at Creative Litho. Likewise, to Jim Konrad and his staff at Creative Label. Also to Patrick O'Connor for all his help and advice through the years. And to Nancy, my wife, for being so supportive and understanding . . .

To **Joe Cirillo,** *a true believer*

"I am a camera with its shutter open, quite passive, recording, not thinking."

—Christopher Isherwood

1

A RAIN CHECK

    I OBSERVED HIM as silently and inconspicuously as a closed circuit camera. He had never been in the shop before nor did he look like a local or tourist. He had thick features and a fleshy face, his kinetic body hunched in a boxer's stance. ZOOM IN FOR A CLOSE-UP . . . His boneless nose lay flat and badly scarred between his bushy eyebrows. He whipped his head from side to side as his deep-set blue eyes scanned the video tape cardboard sleeves on the shelves. He moved his purplish lips while he read the titles. ZOOM OUT FOR A LONG SHOT . . . He was just under six feet tall and was dressed in baggy gray pinstripe trousers and a blue dress shirt. A cotton handkerchief was draped across his shirt collar resting against his red chafed neck. Wearing black wingtipped shoes, he shifted his weight from one foot to the other as he took an inventory of my collection. Through it all he was totally oblivious to my presence.

    I sat on the stool behind the counter. This stranger was my first customer of the day. It was a warm crisp morning, the sun's stark rays streaking through the storefront windows. This would be a slow day. On rainy days my video rental store was packed with disgruntled tourists—spending over a hundred bucks a day to be stuck indoors wasn't their idea of a vacation.

After bouncing off all the walls, he strolled over to me. The man eyed the sign above the counter. It listed the rental rates and membership plans. Thirty dollars for a seasonal membership and one hundred dollars for a lifetime.

"A *lifetime* membership." He read aloud.

"That's right." I said. "It's a good deal. My competitor over on Newtown charges fifty bucks for only an annual membership."

"It sure sounds like a good deal." He said, clearing his throat. "But one thing bothers me."

"Oh?"

"This lifetime membership." He ran his pudgy fingers through his thinning gray hair. "*Whose* lifetime we talkin' about here—yours, mine, or the fuckin' store's?"

My mouth dropped open. The man's agrestic tone and mannerisms startled me for a few seconds. A tough guy from another era with a strong Boston accent. Not since I quit the force had I come across such a hard-boiled type. "Ah—that's a good question."

"Bet nobody's ever asked you that before—am I right?" He asked with a toothy grin.

"Can't say . . ."

"It's a pretty good question—ain't it?" He persisted.

"Yes, it certainly is."

"Well?"

"Huh?" I felt like I was missing something here.

"So what's the dope?" He threw his chin out. "Whose lifetime?"

"The store's, of course." I said matter-of-factly.

"The store's lifetime?"

"Why yes."

"Then this lifetime membership of yours could be a gamble."

"How do you figure that?" I queried.

"You could go out of biz in six months." His eyes widened for emphasis.

"Not with the kind of business I've been doing." I smirked.

"That good, huh?"

"Great . . . just great."

"You sign up all those people, take their hunnert bucks, close shop and split. I like it. It's a good deal all right—for *you*." He laughed.

"It's not like that at all." I shook my head.

"Can you guarantee me that?"

"For a lousy hundred bucks?"

"That ain't cheap." He said seriously.

"You spend that kind of change for a decent meal in this town."

"Not where *I* go."

I grinned. "Well . . . yeah . . . right." I said under my breath.

"Whaddaya mean by that?" He asked defensively, the blood rushing to his face.

"Huh?"

"The wisecrack."

"What wisecrack?"

"That business about 'yeah . . . right'." His face was beet red now, teeth glaring.

"That wasn't a crack."

"How long do you expect to stay in business with an attitude like yours?"

I stood up to emphasize my six-foot-two-inch towering frame. "Hey now, wait a second here."

"You young people are all the same!" He spit out.

"I think you're blowing this all out of proportion." I attempted to calm him down.

"I don't think so."

"Listen, I apologize if you read me wrong."

"I know how to read!" He snapped.

"Hey, tell you what, I'll give you a freebie." I gave him my car salesman's smile.

"What?"

"A tape of your choice. You can rent any tape in my shop for one night on me."

The man looked around and thought it over. "Could I get a rain check on that?"

I stepped back, unable to conceal my reaction. "A *rain check*?"

"Yeah, I don't have a VCR yet, but when I do, can I come back here and take you up on your offer?"

I looked away and muttered under my breath. *I don't believe this asshole*!

"Excuse me?"

"Sure." I swallowed my anger. "After you get your machine, come on in."

The stranger nodded and turned away.

I watched him leave the shop. "'*Whose lifetime are we talking about*?'" I said through clenched teeth. If he ever comes in here again he'll have the shortest membership on record—he'll never make it out the door alive!

I collapsed onto the stool with a long sigh.

It was going to be one of those days. It had started out badly. It was obviously going to get worse. . . .

I woke up this morning feeling shitty and hung over. Jesse and I had hit the clubs last night. That was not the easiest thing to do out here on the East End. You had to contend with a lot of teeny-boppers. Afterwards, we finished off a bottle of Jack Daniel's and made love. I remembered seeing the bedside clock's green digital numbers glaring at me before I shut my eyes: *4:18*.

The next thing I heard was Phil Collins singing on the radio. It took me a few minutes to pry open an eyelid to see the clock radio. *6:37*.

I rolled onto my back and felt for Jesse next to me.

She was gone but the sheet was still warm.

Monday morning. She was off to the city for the week.

I sat up and caught her as she was coming out of the bathroom after a brisk shower. She was naked, her breasts bobbing with every step. Her golden wisps of genital hair glowed against her damp tawny skin. Just three hours before such a sight would have sent blood rushing to my loins, but now I looked upon her without passion. Indeed, it was the morning after.

She leaned over and pecked me listlessly on the lips. Cool drops of water fell from her wet curly blond locks to my chest, piercing me like needles. There were dark puffy crescents under her eyes.

"Go back to sleep." She said in a whisper and shut off the clock radio. Phil Collins faded away.

"Jesus—how do you do it?" I asked with a groggy mumble. "Two hours sleep."

She smiled. She *always* had a smile for me. I used to have to twist my ex's arm just to get to see her teeth once in awhile.

"I have to catch the train."

She went to her dresser and pulled open the top drawer. She picked out a pair of white cotton briefs and slipped them on.

I watched her dress. Her whole body was tanned— no bikini lines—the virtues of owning a secluded acre of land.

She noticed that I was staring at her. "Go back to bed."

"I don't feel so good." I held my stomach and made a sour face.

"A rough night."

"Barely remember it." I rubbed the sleep from my eyes.

"Do you recall the night cap?" She gave me her crooked grin.

I managed a smirk.

"Do you remember *what* you said?"

I shrugged. "I said something?" I looked down at my toes poking out of the sheet at the foot of the bed.

She shook her head. "Go back to sleep."

She slipped into a bra, clutching it in the front. When she realized that I was still watching her she swung around and put her back to me. "*Always* staring . . ."

"You pissed or something?" I asked.

"I have to catch a train." She adjusted the broad shoulder pads under her white Norma Kamali dress. "I'll call you later at the shop." She leaned over to peck me again. This time I pulled her down on me. I kissed her firmly on the lips.

"Mitch—my dress!"

I smelled toothpaste on her breath.

"Later . . ." She said and stood up, adjusting herself.

"Alright . . . what did I do now?"

"Nothing, Mitch." She sounded hassled. "You stink of booze."

"I thought we had a good time." I glanced away showing her that I was hurt by her cold shoulder routine.

"We did."

I looked her in the eye. Jesus, even without makeup she was beautiful. "I don't get it."

"Just keep *it* in your pants this week, okay?" She said firmly.

"Is that what I promised?"

"Just chill-out, Mitch." She hurried out the door. "I'll call you later."

"Yeah, later." I said indignantly.

Women had this problem with infidelity. They didn't like it when their men got the itch. I had been pretty loyal these last few months. She must've heard a rumor in town. We've been at it for over two years now. What else did she want from me?

Besides *that*.

I had made that mistake once before. It had been a disaster. Never again, I had promised myself. Although Jesse was special I wasn't prepared to renege on my declaration. My only peeve about her was her jealousy. I had fallen in love with her the first time I spotted her on the tube doing a designer jean commercial. She was an actress. Jesse Dillon. She was good, but she got bogged down doing commercials and soaps. Her newest gig was the voice for Mikey the Beaver on a Saturday morning cartoon program. It wasn't the kind of stuff that thrilled her, but the big bucks helped her cope with it . . .

A face in the window sucked me back into reality. It was a teenager. He had a carrot-colored crew cut and vampire white skin. Dressed in an oversized Day-Glo orange shirt and black baggy pants, he stood motionless before the storefront looking at himself in the monitor. I had set up a video cam in the window so people could look at themselves. It was a crowd-stopper. People liked looking at themselves nowadays. He looked like a refugee from the East Village but he actually lived out here most of the year—a hundred miles from Alphabet City.

He had an extraordinary face—high cheekbones, azure eyes, milky complexion—he was almost pretty. He hung outside the store a lot . . . looking at himself. He had never once ventured inside. He would tell his mother what he wanted and she would come in and get it. Mostly offbeat fare like *Liquid Sky*. His old lady was a looker. The other side of forty but she still had *it*. Rita Hayworth hair, a trim, shapely bod, and an incredible pair of baby blue peepers that hit me every time she entered the store. Her name was Nicola Gage.

Nicola. I liked it. I liked her. She liked me. I thought about it a few times, but I wanted her to make the first move. A safety precaution to make sure we were on the same frequency. Otherwise it would be bad for business if it ever came out that I was seducing my customers.

And there she was standing next to the crew cut kid. She was wearing a white polo shirt—dark circles beneath—and white tennis shorts. She wore her hair shoulder length. It was silky and shimmering. She nodded to the boy and entered the store. She came towards me with her tennis racket tucked under her arm, barely a wrinkle on her beautiful tanned face.

I stood up to greet her.

She returned my smile. "Good afternoon, Jeff."

"Hi."

"Not too bad in here today."

"It's the good weather—bad for business."

She gave me the once-over. "Did *The Big Chill* come back yet?"

I shook my head. "I have you on the reservation list—it's still a popular movie after all this time."

"Tell me about it." She smirked. "It must be the Yuppies' favorite movie."

"As soon as it comes in, it's yours, Mrs. Gage."

"Thank you. Oh, do you have *Repo Man*?"

"*Who?*"

"*Repo Man*."

"Ah." I shot a glance at her son in the window. "Not *Liquid Sky* again?"

"Ten times is enough for that kid." She shook her head. "By the way, what is this *Repo Man*?"

"A West Coast version of *Liquid Sky*."

"Natch." She smiled.

I went out to the science fiction case and found the

tape. "You're lucky it's in. This movie has a cult following . . . "

I came around the counter and caught her checking out the 'Adults Only' section. "Can I help you with anything else?"

"Ah . . . well I've been having problems with my VCR." She said nervously.

"Oh?"

"Yeah—I've been getting a fuzzy picture and the sound just isn't right."

"Probably need to clean your . . . heads." I said with a grin, my eyes burning into hers.

"I wish you could look at it." She broke away from our trance. "My husband usually handles these things but he's away this week."

"Oh?"

"On business." She explained.

I played dumb. "You could bring it in . . . I can't promise you anything—I'm not a repairman, y'know."

"I don't know, Jeff . . . the wires and all . . . couldn't you come out and take a look?"

I couldn't restrain myself—I beamed brightly. "Well . . . I don't know. I'm here 'til nine."

"I could fix you a late dinner. I mean, for your trouble." She wet her lips.

I cleared my throat. "I guess it'll be okay . . . if it's not too late?"

Now *she* smiled. "I never hit the sack before midnight." She purred.

"Okay." I nodded. "You got yourself a deal."

"Great . . . I really appreciate it."

"No problem." I wrote out her receipt and she hurried out of the shop.

I sat down on the stool with a big smile on my puss.

Maybe it wasn't going to be one of those days after all.

2

SCREEN TEST

THE EAST END of Long Island was a virtual playland for the rich and famous . . . and for everybody else, if they could afford it. The average income was one of the highest in the whole nation. Once a secluded rural area for artists and writers who lived among the local fishermen, the Hamptons have since become upscaled and over-developed.

I used to come out here as a kid with my family. We would rent a cottage for two weeks in the Maidstone Park area. Swim and fish. It was like the Fresh Air Fund for a Brooklyn-bred family. Nowadays it would be impossible for a low-income family to afford the outrageous rental rates.

I was thinking about how much it had all changed in the past two decades as I drove my black Porsche to Nicola's house. She lived in nearby Springs, an area known for its art galleries. It was a mixed area. Some artists. Some wealth. Some local have-nots. I pulled into her driveway and parked behind her Mercedes convertible.

It was too dark to really check out her house. But it appeared large and was certainly expensive. I hit the doorbell and watched the mosquitoes swarming around the dim yellow lamp as I waited. In a few moments the door opened and there she was.

Nicola ushered me into the house and quickly shut the door. She worked me over with her baby blues as she stood there wrapped in a silver satin robe, her hands on her hips. The next line usually went: "How about a drink?" And I would say, "Sounds good to me." "What'll it be—scotch?" She'd ask. And I would gulp loudly and nod my head like a bashful schoolboy. But she didn't even ask. The silence was killing me so I said, "Nice place."

She said, "Thank you." More eye-work.

I had raced through the afternoon and evening just thinking about tonight. But here we were and tension was in the air. I felt very awkward standing there. Like maybe I got her vibes all wrong and she really wanted me to fix her goddamn VCR. But then I gave her the once-over, real slow, and knew we were on the same wavelength.

She smiled. "This way . . . dinner's almost ready."

I followed her into the kitchen. She had a big pot going with boiling water. "You like pasta?"

"My favorite." I said as I put down a bottle of wine and a videotape cleaner on the table. "Red—I guessed right."

She smiled and ran her tongue across her teeth.

I gulped loudly. We were definitely on the same wavelength.

She carefully put the fresh linguine into the pot. "I make my own tomato sauce—I hope you like it." She began stirring the bubbling sauce as it cooked on the stove.

"Can I help you with anything?" I asked sheepishly.

She eyed me with a grin. "Just open the wine—let it breathe for awhile."

"Sure." I went to work. "Didn't realize you would go to so much trouble for dinner."

"It's no trouble."

"You would make someone a great wife." I quipped.

"You should remind my husband of that." She said seriously.

"Trouble in paradise?"

Nicola stopped what she was doing and swung around to face me. No words just a look. And what a look. I knew it was time to change the subject.

I cleared my throat and said, "It sure smells great."

She nodded with a slight smile, taking note of my not very clever aversion, then went back to her cooking.

I stood there in the kitchen awkwardly. "Maybe I should look at your VCR while you prepare dinner?"

"It can wait."

"Okay." She was obviously running the show.

"Besides dinner's almost done. Would you mind draining the pot?"

"Sure." I ventured over to the electric range and picked up the hefty cookware with pot holders. I began pouring the boiling water into the colander in the sink. The steam blew back at me, giving me an unwanted facial.

She put the linguine into a large bowl and mixed in the sauce. "You bring the wine."

I followed her into the dining room. We sat down to eat.

"I hope you're hungry." She said.

"Haven't eaten anything since this morning."

"Then you must be starving."

I shrugged. "I could stand to lose a few pounds."

She gave me her look and remarked, "I don't think so—you look terrific!"

"You're embarrassing me." I poured the wine.

"You should be proud of your body." She said seductively. "I know I'm proud of mine."

"Now you're talking about something to be proud of." I winked.

She brought the pasta to her mouth and began to chew, the tomato sauce dripping down her chin. She extended her tongue to lap it up.

"Do you like?" She inquired.

"Love it." I replied although I was too entranced watching her eat to notice the food.

This went on for an eternity. We exchanged some gossip but my interest lay elsewhere.

Finally we finished dinner. I stood up and began to clear the table.

"Don't bother." She said as she wiped her mouth. "My maid will take care of that in the morning."

"Sounds good to me."

"Now about my sick VCR."

"Yeah . . . where's the patient?"

She smiled and said, "It's in my bedroom."

I followed her past the spacious kitchen, through a hallway, closed doors whipping by, until we entered the master bedroom. It was big. A large round bed covered in white fur in the center. Mirrors all over the place. A 25-inch monitor just before the bed. A VCR on top. An autofocus video camcorder on a tripod next to that. Quite a set up. She went to the VCR and switched it on. The monitor came to life and there was an image of Nicola laying on the bed. She was naked and on her back, knees in the air, her hand at her crotch. The soundtrack was her sighing. "See all this static?"

To tell you the truth, I didn't notice any noise bars. I couldn't keep my eyes off the image on the screen. "Not bad."

"I find it annoying." She complained.

"Could use a cleaning." I gave her my professional opinion.

"Well, you brought the equipment."

I looked away from the set and into her eyes. "That I did."

I shut off the machine and ejected the tape. I popped in the cleaner cassette and ran it through the machine once. "That should do it."

She put in a fresh cassette and switched it on to record. She turned on the camera and the empty bed appeared on the screen. "Let's test it."

She pushed me onto the bed and removed her robe. She was naked beneath. I saw the rear view on the monitor. I didn't know where to look—at her in the flesh or on the TV set. My eyes were drawn to the screen. She began removing my clothes. I watched it all on the monitor. Soon I was as naked as she was. She lay on top of me. All this was happening much too fast for me.

"I could use another drink." I said, revealing my apprehension.

She pushed her hair back. "A drink?" She asked in puzzlement.

"Just to put me in the mood." I rationalized. Never mind I just drank half a bottle of wine! Even though all systems were ready to go, I had a last minute guilt attack. It had been some time since I screwed around behind Jesse's back. I flashed on her from this morning. *Just keep it in your pants*, she had said. I wondered if she was psychic!

Nicola rolled off me and searched for something in the bedside table. She pulled out a mirror and a plastic bag. "This oughta do it."

She spread out four short lines on the mirror and took a snort through a thin straw. I leaned over and inhaled a line. "Haven't done this in ages."

"Really?" She looked at me in disbelief. I guess I wasn't as hip as she thought.

"Uh-huh."

"Why's that?" She asked.

"I don't know . . . Jack delivers a better state of mind." I told her.

"Jack—who's Jack?"

"Old buddy of mine . . . Jack Daniel's." I smiled. She grinned. "We might have some in the bar."

"Where's that?" I eyeballed the room.

She pointed in back of me. "Behind that wall."

Now I grinned. "Quite a place you have here."

"I heard you have a high-tech number yourself."

"Well, I'm into electronics." I stood up and went to the mirrored wall. I looked silly standing there in my birthday suit. "What do I do?"

"Just push." She instructed.

I pushed the wall and it swung around. A wet bar

magically appeared before me. I laughed. "I like it."
I immediately spotted the black and white label. I
poured myself a glass on the rocks. "You want
anything?"

"Just you, baby." She patted the bed.

I watched myself on the tube as I rejoined her.
"Can't say I ever did this before in front of a camera."

"I thought you said you were into electronics."
She winked.

We snickered.

"How did you hear about my house?" I asked.

"I heard a lot of things about you."

"Oh?"

"You're an ex-cop." She said, giving me a side-
ways glance.

"Brave of you to be snorting that stuff in front of
me knowing that."

"I said you were an *ex*-cop." She accentuated.

"Cops are like Catholics . . . once a cop always a
cop." I declared.

She grinned sardonically. "Besides, I bought some
of my best coke from cops."

I nodded. "I bet."

"I also heard you won the lottery."

"Y'know what the odds were . . . ?"

"You split from the force and bought an old house
out here on an acre of land. You refurbished it. You
opened that video shop just to keep from getting
bored. You collect eighty-something thou a year from
your winnings alone. That'll keep coming in for
twenty years." She leaned over the mirror plate, her
red hair covering her face, and snorted the last two
lines. She came up, her eyes closed, her hair in

disarray. She cleared her throat, opened her eyes, and continued on with her dossier on me. As she spoke the muscles in my stomach tightened. "You drive around in a ten year old Porsche Targa convertible. You spend some time with a model/actress named Jesse Dillon. You're divorced. You have a reputation with the ladies I haven't been able to verify . . . *yet.*"

I sat up, feeling even more naked than before. "What did you do—hire a private dick for chrissakes?"

She stretched out on the bed. "I just like to know who I'm sleeping with—that's all."

"I don't have herpes—if that's what you're worried about!" I got up from the bed and drained my glass. She sure knew how to blow my mood. My boner took a nosedive.

She came after me. "I'm sorry."

"I have this thing about people checking me out—I get enough of that shit from the creditors, thank you." I walked away from her.

"I said I was sorry." She pleaded.

"*No*body goes to such extremes to dig into somebody's private affairs just to hop in the sack with him." I said, taking her in with an accusing glance.

"I was only kidding about that . . . everybody knows about you . . . this is a small town." She made it sound like we had been talking about my cow giving birth to a calf or some other idle gossip.

"Well, don't believe everything you hear, sweetheart." I snapped.

"Hey, you're really pissed off." She observed as though she had only now figured out I don't like being put under the microscope.

"No shit." I said sarcastically. "I could use another drink." I returned to the bar.

"I apologize . . . I didn't know you were so sensitive." She remarked softly.

I filled my glass and took it all in one swig. "Well, we know *you're* not the sensitive one here."

She came up to the bar. "Hey, let's start all over again—okay?"

I shrugged. "What about your son—is he home?"

"My what?" She asked. "What're you talking about?"

"Your kid—the *Repo Man*."

She covered her mouth and laughed.

"I don't get the joke." I said.

She fell onto the bed still in hysterics.

"I SAID I DON'T GET IT!" I shouted and slammed the glass onto the bar counter.

She stopped and looked me in the eye. "You're pretty high-strung."

"I just want to know what's so funny?" I inquired frankly.

She sobered up and asserted, "I don't have a son."

"Then who's the orange-haired kid?" I poured another drink.

"Chloe—my daughter."

"Your daughter?" I asked in disbelief.

"Yes." She smiled.

"Jesus . . . now I'm sorry." I shook my head, feeling the fool for my outburst. "I was getting worried there for awhile . . . thought I was going queer or something."

"Well, hands off, Mitchum—she's only fifteen." She warned, her maternal instincts aroused.

"Jail bait." I laid down next to her.

"Can we get on with this now?" She asked.

I finished my drink and looked at us in the monitor. "Yeah, sure, we're in the middle of a test— aren't we?"

3

BEDSIDE COMPANION

I HEARD SOMETHING in my sleep. A clicking noise then a whirring sound. I slowly peeled back my eyelids. I saw a white ceiling. But it didn't look like the white ceiling of my bedroom. I sat up and saw myself on the monitor. The VCR was rewinding the tape—an automatic feature when a cassette runs to the end. That must have been the sound I heard. I lay back on the pillow and glanced over at Nicola. A glint of light washed over us from the bedside lamp. Her eyes were staring at me in a fixed gaze. She was perfectly still and expressionless. There was a blond wooden handle with a metal cap sticking out of her ear. Still sluggish, it took a few seconds to sink in. Then I shot up, my eyes never leaving her face. My heart pounding in my ears.

"Nicola?" I walked around the bed to her side and leaned over. I immediately recognized what the handle belonged to. The last time I had seen one was inside a blood-stained plastic bag as evidence. It was an ice pick. I didn't even know why I bothered to check her pulse—she was dead alright. Her body was still warm. Blood oozed from her ear. The attack must've just occurred minutes before. I took in a deep breath to settle my nerves. Cool down. You're a pro, I kept telling myself. I've seen this dozens of times before. A dead body. A murder victim. But this time it was different. Because this time I was there when it happened. In fact, I could be considered a suspect. I gave the place a quick once-over. My fingerprints were all over the place. I had to think fast. Call the police? What do I tell them? That I woke up in a strange woman's bed and found her dead beside me? What about the truth. We had fucked all night then fell asleep—I woke up and she didn't? I paced the floor nervously. This looked like an obvious frame job. It certainly wasn't a crime of passion. Her irate husband didn't come home and find us and stab her in the ear with the first sharp object he could find. This job was much too clean.

The VCR clicked again and I went to it. The tape was wound. That was it! The tape—the killer might be on it. In order to be certain, I would have to run through the full two hours of tape. I turned around and eyed the body. No, I really didn't want to stick around here messing with her tape deck. I'd rather play it on my more sophisticated equipment. I guess I just wanted to get the hell out of there as soon as possible! I began to get dress. I thought it through as I hurriedly slipped into my clothes. I would stop by the shop and search through the tape there. If the killer was on the tape, I would take it and a portable VCR to the police station and play it for them.

After dressing, I stood at the foot of the bed and

looked at her body. I still couldn't figure it out. Why her and not *me*? Why not both of us? What was going on here?

I left the house and walked to the driveway. My convertible sat there in the darkness, the full moon high in the cobalt blue sky. I hopped over the top and into the seat. The engine turned over without a hitch. I pulled out of the long driveway leaving her red Mercedes behind. The air was cool and damp and felt good flowing over me. I sucked in deeply, clearing my head. I got onto Springs-Fireplace Road and drove straight into town. The traffic wasn't bad this time of night. A few teenagers in their daddies' cars trying to outwit the local police—no mean feat. When I stopped at the intersection, I saw two fire trucks a few blocks up ahead in vicinity of my store. There were a lot of flashing lights and gawking spectators. I waited until the light changed and drove by the commotion.

It *was* my store!

I pulled over behind a patrol car and ran to the storefront. Smoke was still in the air. The fire chief, Jake Hayden, was at the doorway.

"Well, there you are, Mitchum." Hayden took off his helmet and wiped the sweat from his brow. "Tried calling you at home."

"What the hell . . ." I stood there with a gaping mouth.

"You were lucky—not much damage. A kid spotted the blaze and called us."

I entered the store and was overwhelmed by the smoky stench. The back wall was charred and in ruins.

"Started in the rear room . . . still checking out the cause." Hayden put his arm around me. "You okay, Mitchum?"

"I don't believe this . . ." I said with a trembling voice.

"Most of the tapes and hardware are okay." Hayden walked around. "Just some smoke and water damage."

I stood there in distress, my mind reeling. First the murder and now this. I'd heard of bad luck streaks— but this was going too far!

"Best thing for you is to go home and hit the sack. Worry about this mess in the morning." Hayden patted me on the back. I looked into his pale blue eyes. He was okay. We had a mutual understanding. He had come out of the Bronx after twenty years in the department. That was a long time to spend putting out fires in that hellhole. He had seen everything there. And with my years as an undercover cop, well, we had an understanding. At least I thought so at the time.

"Yeah, I guess you're right, Hayden." In a trance, I walked out the door, past the firefighters and pedestrians, and slipped into my car. I gripped the steering wheel and brought my face down against my arms.

It ended up being one of those days after all.

4

RERUNS

REWIND. STOP. PLAY. Jesse
and me watching television in the living room of her
Manhattan apartment. It was Indian Summer—the air
conditioner buzzing in the middle of October. The
intercom rang. Jesse gave me the eye. I didn't see it;
I felt it. My own eyes were glued to the tube. I was
watching J.R. Ewing giving Cliff Barnes a hard time
on *Dallas*. Video junk food. I was hooked. She
sighed and went to the intercom. She asked the doorman, a Cuban with a thick accent and even thicker
bandit mustache, who was calling. His voice crack-
led over the speaker. I didn't catch the name. Jesse
told him to send the person up. She walked back into
the room and plopped down on the couch. "It's for
you." She informed me. "Adam."

"Adam?" I tore myself away from the screen.
"What does *he* want?"

She pretended to ignore me.

I got up and went to the door. I opened it and
looked out into the empty hall. I stood there and
waited.

27

Adam Hayes was my boss. I had just given notice of my retirement from the force thanks to my good fortune with the lottery. I thought he was there to try and talk me out of it.

The elevator arrived and Adam swaggered out. He was big and black with close-cropped hair and mustache. He was dressed in a brown suit and pink shirt, a loose tie around his neck. He came up to the doorway looking more tired than usual. He leaned up against the wall just outside the door.

"Adam." I smiled.

"Mitch." He said sadly.

"Come on in." I offered.

He didn't budge. "Jesse inside?"

I nodded.

"Then we better stay out here." He sighed.

I stared deeply into his black eyes. "I told you, man, I'm splittin'. There's no way you're going to talk me out of it."

He dismissed me with a wave of his hand. "When was the last time you saw Kate?"

"Kate?" I had just had dinner with my ex-wife. "Last week—why?"

Adam took a deep breath then let it come out slowly. "I'm sorry, Mitch."

My heart missed a beat.

"Just came from her place." Adam shifted his weight from one foot to the other. "A neighbor called us when she noticed the door was ajar."

"Burglary?"

Adam nodded. "We found her on the bed. D.O.A. Found this on the floor nearby." He reached into his pocket and pulled out a plastic bag. Inside the blood-soaked sack was an ice pick. "The place is a mess. Need you to take a look . . . see what's missing."

I looked down. I didn't know what to say . . . I didn't even know how to feel.

"I'm so sorry, Mitch." He conveyed with his sad puppy eyes.

"Thanks for telling me in person." I had trouble looking him in the eye.

"You okay?" He held my arm.

"I guess I can't win. I'm quitting the fuckin' force to get away from it. Poor Kate." I shook my head and hissed. "She was getting her act together. The divorce had given her a whole new lease on life. Too bad it was so short. She deserved more, so much more."

"Come on, Mitch, these things happen." Stated the jaded cop.

"Yeah, but they're supposed to happen to someone *else*." I was losing it. A dry lump as big as a plum pit lodged in my throat.

"You better get dressed." Adam said.

I glanced down at myself and realized I was wearing a tee-shirt and sweats.

I went into the apartment and came face-to-face with Jesse. She stood there. She must've overheard our conversation. Tears welled up in her eyes. She said, "I'm sorry, Mitch."

I opened my mouth but nothing came out.

I got dressed and left with Adam. We didn't say a word to one another during the drive. We pulled up behind a double-parked patrol car, it's party-hat flashing. An ambulance was just driving off.

Adam turned off the engine and faced me. Our eyes locked. ''If you can't go through with this . . .''

''Come on, Adam, I'm a cop.'' I declared.

''Not for long . . .'' He reminded me.

''You still pissed because I'm trading in my badge?'' I inquired, detecting an undertone of resentment.

''You were the best, Mitch.'' He complimented me.

''That's what they all say.'' I got out of the car. The air was thick and stagnant. I felt like I had gained twenty pounds.

Adam shot me a glance across the top of the car. ''Do you believe this heat?''

''I guess I'll have to identify the body down at the morgue.'' The thought unnerved me.

''Her folks are down there right at this moment.'' Adam related as he walked around the car to join me.

''How did she look?'' I asked gravely, expecting to hear the worst.

''Like she was asleep. It was a clean job . . . no chopped meat.'' Adam conveyed in his policeman's monotone.

''Where?''

''In the ear . . .'' He stuck his finger in his ear to show me.

''She didn't feel a thing then.'' An ice pick through the ear meant instant brain death.

''She was asleep when it happened . . . she still had on her nightgown.'' He said, adding, ''Nothing kinky—it wasn't a sex crime.''

''The apartment a mess?'' I asked, flashing on Kate's immaculate white-on-white apartment.

He nodded. ''Yep, she lost a lot of blood.''

I swallowed hard.

Adam hoisted his trousers. "Let's do it."

I followed him into the building.

A red stain like an ink blotch covered the upper part of the bed sheets. Kate had never used a pillow, complaining it screwed up her neck. An outline of her body was taped on the bed. The entire studio apartment was a shambles. Broken glass, shredded clothes, and books spewed everywhere.

They were still dusting for fingerprints.

I eyed Adam. "No one heard this?" I asked incredulously.

"We're knocking on doors now."

"I want this case." I announced unequivocally.

Adam shook his head. "No way. Besides you quit—remember?"

I pushed my face against his like a bulldog, our noses almost touching. "I said I *want* it!"

"You're off the force, Mitch."

"Then I'll do it without the force. One way or another, I'm going after the animal who did this!" I threatened.

Adam put his heavy hand on my shoulder. "This is no good, man. Take it easy. Remember you're a pro."

I swung around, my eyes on the ceiling. "This is personal."

"Exactly." Adam said.

I faced him. "I have to, Adam. She was my wife . . . I owe her. I'm a goddamn cop."

"Not anymore. You seem to keep forgetting that." Adam kept reminding me. "Hell, I would love you to change your mind. But not for this reason. Besides the brass would never allow it. And anyway, you're an undercover cop. You know the street scene, not how to conduct a murder investigation. This is way out of your league, Mitch.''

"Then who's going to handle this case?''

"Bobby.''

I hissed a complaint. "That *schmuck*.''

"It's his!'' Adam made it loud and clear.

I shook my head as I eyed the outline of her body on the bloody sheets. "I'm going to find this scumbag. He's dead.'' I faced Adam. "*Dead*!''

STOP. FAST FORWARD. PLAY.

I sat up in bed. My body soaked from sweat. I kicked away the sheet. The chilled air from the ceiling vent gave me goose-bumps. I swung my feet around and placed them on the carpeted floor. I rubbed my eyes. The house in silence. The room glowing from the razor-sharp sunlight that poured from the skylight.

I wondered . . . hoped . . . that it was all a dream . . . a nightmare. But no, it all came back to me. That scene from two years ago. And the horror show that had taken place only a few hours ago. I stood up. My naked body was trim and tanned. A healthy body. A few aches and pains now and then, but I had no complaints. I went into the bathroom and turned on the shower. Ice cold water. I stepped inside the tub. I almost screamed from the pain. But I gripped my jaw and held my stance. I had to be sure that I was wide-awake. I shut the faucets off and stepped onto the tiled floor. I patted myself dry with the bath sheet. I stood before the mirror above the sink and prepared to shave. I lathered up my face with the brush and was about to start when I heard the door-bell. I washed off the soap and put on my terry cloth robe. I hurried down the stairs to the front door and halted. My hand froze on the doorknob.

Could this be the local police?

I took in a deep breath and opened the door. Hayden dressed casually in jeans and a knit polo shirt stood before me.

I exhaled.

"Good afternoon, Mitchum."

"Is it afternoon, already?" I waved him inside.

"Just past one." He related. "Hope I'm not disturbing you."

I shook my head. "Just got out of the shower. Come in and sit down." We went into the media room and sat down on the black leather sofa. On the adjacent wall sat a Mitsubishi thirty-five inch television set and shelves packed with various electronic components.

"Nice set-up you got here." Hayden looked over my equipment. "Looks like something out of one of those *Star Wars* pictures."

"Thank you." I gazed over at the bar. "How 'bout a drink?"

"No, thanks." He declined. He was a good thirty pounds overweight with his belly protruding over his NYFD belt buckle.

"What brings you out here?"

"It's about your shop."

"The fire?"

"Yes." He was perspiring nervously, dark rings forming around his underarms.

"I appreciate the fine work you and your men did to try and save my store." I told him gratefully.

"That's our job." Hayden cleared his throat. "I found out the cause."

"Oh?"

"Yes." He gave me a penetrating look. "It was arson."

"Arson?" I stood up. "Are you serious?"

"I assume you didn't have any knowledge of it?" He inquired as he gazed up at me.

"Arson . . . I don't believe it." I chopped the air with my hand.

"It was a professional job. I've seen work like this before. We didn't get many clean-cut jobs in the Bronx . . . but I still picked up a few tricks of the trade." He wiped his sweaty brow.

I rubbed my forehead. "I swear to you, I had no knowledge of any arson. I mean, I love that store. I was making a fortune."

"That's what I thought." He said with a hint of distrust in his voice.

"Who the hell would torch my shop?" I was furious.

"That's why I came to see you first. I haven't filed a report yet. This won't look good for you with the insurance company." He contended confidentially.

"No, of course it won't." I sat down again. "Thank you. But could you give me some time before you file. I have to get to the bottom of this. Some strange shit's been going on."

"I don't know how long I can put it off. Are you going to ask some of your old buddies for help?" He asked.

"Old buddies? Oh, you mean from the force. Yeah—that's a good idea."

He eyed me suspiciously. "You wouldn't be bullshitting me, would you?"

"Huh? No-no. I didn't torch the shop. Please believe me." I expressed sincerely.

"You haven't received any threats? Perhaps vengeance from someone you put away?" He appeared genuinely concerned.

I shrugged. "I haven't heard a thing. Everything was going just fine. Then it all turned into a bad dream."

"Well, I think I can trust you, Mitchum." He stood up. "But I do have to file shortly. I mean, I don't want to get into any hot water over this." He said with a trembling voice.

"I understand that. Just give me some time . . . just enough for me to uncover the truth." I took him in. He was shaking like a leaf. I realized I couldn't depend on him for too long before he broke down.

"I'll do my best." He offered.

I took his hand. "Thanks again."

"Keep in touch, okay?"

"Sure." I walked him to the door.

He stepped outside and put on his baseball cap. "I know you haven't been here long, Mitchum, but this is basically a tourist town. We like to keep it clean and simple."

"I understand that."

"People want to come out here to relax. To get *away* from the filth of city life. I hope you didn't bring some of that dirt with you when you moved out here. I've been here for over ten years now. I left it all behind. I know it isn't easy, but it just doesn't belong out here." He was getting over his nervousness very quickly.

"What are you driving at, Hayden?" I resented his tone of voice.

"I know about cops. Especially you undercover types. There's a thin line between the good and the bad guys. Sometimes, one rubs off onto the other. Do you get my drift?" He arched his eyebrows.

"I get it but I don't know why I'm gettin' it." I said defensively.

"Just want to clear the air, Mitchum. I'll do you a favor but if I find out you're somehow involved . . ." He was too scared to sound threatening.

"I got the message." I made him feel my anger.

"Have a nice day, Mr. Mitchum." He wandered off with a limp wave of his hand.

"Yeah." I said and shut the door after the little weasel.

5

SNUFF VIDEO

I WATCHED NICOLA push me back onto the bed and remove her robe. The tape quality wasn't bad. But with the low resolution and poor lighting, it came off like a cheapo porn movie. I relived the night before as the images played on my television screen. The sounds. The voices. Our voices. My voice. And a dead woman's. It didn't seem like it had just happened a few hours ago. And having it on tape made it seem all the more real. Even more realistic than real life. That was the strange thing about the electronic image. It wasn't real until you saw the grainy images on the tube. If it happened on TV, it had to be the truth. It was like the CNN news team had been at the scene. I could imagine the media bidding on this tape. An exclusive. An actual murder on the six o'clock news. They could have instant replays in slow motion.

I pressed the remote fast forward scan. The night played on in comical, jerky fast speed. It reminded me of that fast motion orgy scene in *A Clockwork Orange*. The old in-out, in-out. Our bodies jumping

37

around all the corners of the bed. I paused a few times. A freeze frame of her smiling face. She looked older on tape. The hard lighting and unflinching camera eye capturing every wrinkle. Then the action petered out. We were under the satin sheets. A few moments of sweet talk before we dozed off. I turned a few times. She lay on her back for the most part. Now the tape resembled an early Warhol. It was like watching paint dry. Then it happened.

Nicola rolled onto her side facing me. I was flat on my back. The screen went black for a second as someone passed by the camera. Then I saw the back of the killer. It was a woman with long black hair. She was wearing a bright yellow rain slicker. The type a kid wears. She turned to face the bed. I saw her profile. She was wearing dark Yoko Ono sun shades—Porsche brand. The glasses managed to disguise her face very well. She raised her arm, the ice pick in her vinyl-gloved hand. She leaned forward just a tiny bit, her hair falling across her face. Then she brought her hand down, the sharp instrument entering the ear in one brisk sweep. Nicola's body jerked in a short spasm. The killer straightened up and was about to turn when the tape ended.

Natch.

I rewound the tape to the point where the killer entered. I played it back in slow motion. I froze the image of the killer several times—studying her face. Using my video printer, I burned a few thermal paper prints. The pictures weren't of the highest quality— they were in black and white with a two hundred and forty-line screen—but they would come in handy in trying to detect the identity of the killer.

I leaned back on the sofa, prints in hand, sipping my sour mash. The killer reminded me of someone. The long dark hair. The tight chiseled features . . . Kate. It was a sick joke. My ex-wife, murdered by an ice pick, comes back to life to kill someone else with the same kind of weapon. It was perverse. I had to lay off the juice. But didn't Kate used to have a yellow slicker? Was somebody trying to fuck with my head?

What the hell was going on here?

My own investigation into Kate's death had gone on for months. I was off the force so I was limited. Adam was a great help.

Bobby Finkelstein was another case. He headed the investigation. He managed to pick up one suspect. A black kid with a yellow sheet as long as my arm. Mostly armed robbery. But they didn't have any concrete evidence so they released him.

I met up with him a few days later.

He didn't do it.

It took me a few hours to figure that out. The kid was missing a few teeth and one eye was swollen shut. Maybe some people would consider my tactics excessively brutal. But don't feel too bad for the boy. A month later he was arrested for sticking a screwdriver through an elderly woman's face during a robbery.

I continued to scrutinize the prints. At least I had proof that I did not kill Nicola. That made me feel better. But I still had a lot of other queries. Like who pulled the torch job on my shop? And were the two incidents related? Was somebody out to sabotage me? The questions flooded my brain. I had so little to go on. These prints might prove too fuzzy for a computer comparison check. And what if the killer was in disguise? It could have been a man in drag for all I knew.

I wondered if they found her body yet. If they had, they would have finished dusting by now. Checking on my fingerprints. Doing a blood test of my semen.

I had no choice. I had to go to them. I had the tape to cover my own ass. But of course the newspapers would have a field day. **HAMPTONS' ICE PICK MURDERER ON THE LOOSE** would be the *New York Post* banner. My name would be dragged through the mud. Jesse would leave me. I would have to sell the store and move elsewhere. My whole life destroyed. It would mean starting all over again. And they would play up my ex-wife's murder. An ice pick used in both incidents. Jesus, how could I talk my way out of that one? Coincidental? That was the one thing that plagued me the most. The similarities of the two murders. Was it just a coincidence? Or did somebody do their homework on my background?

Nicola. She seemed to have the lowdown on me. It had unnerved me the way she went on and on about my personal affairs. She had mentioned everything except Kate's murder. Since she had known I was divorced, surely she would have been aware of her death as well.

I went to my VCR and ejected the tape. What choice did I have? I had to go to the police. There was a lot more to this than I suspected. It might have had nothing to do with Nicola at all. It obviously had everything to do with me. I might be in danger at this very moment.

I got dressed promptly. I put on a pair of jeans and

a cotton shirt. It was a hot, humid day. I didn't even bother to shave. I just wanted to get this done.

I hopped into my car and drove into town. Every passing car was suspect. Was I being tailed? It didn't seem like it. My stomach was tied in knots. The tape tucked in my crotch between my legs on the seat. It was the only thing I had and I was petrified of losing it. Maybe the killer knew I had it and she would come for it. My mind reeled on and on . . . filled to capacity, working in overdrive.

I had to stop by the store to pick up a portable VCR player. I pulled into the public parking lot and walked over to the shop. I stopped in my tracks when I saw her. She was waiting outside my storefront, a tape in hand.

It was Chloe.

I swallowed hard and wandered over to her. She was dressed in turquoise balloon pants and a white athletic tee-shirt. No bra. The dark of her nipples showed through. She craned her head to look at me, her eyes squinting in the sharp sunlight. I peered at her through my black Ray-Bans.

"What happened to your store?" She asked in a husky mature voice that didn't seem to fit her youthfulness.

It took me awhile to get the words out. "A fire." It was so obvious an answer but I was still getting over the shock of seeing her there.

"I'm returning your tape." She held up the case to show me.

I wondered when she had the chance to view it—she certainly hadn't watched it in her mom's bedroom. "Did you like?"

She nodded.

"How 'bout your mom—she like it?" I inquired.

She laughed. "My mother never watches this stuff."

"How is your mom?" Pressing her on.

"Okay . . . I guess."

"You guess?"

"Yeah."

"Doesn't she usually bring back the tapes? In fact, I don't even remember you ever coming into my shop." I was beginning to sound like a cop again.

She looked down. "I have . . . a few times."

"Your mom playing tennis?" I wanted so much to hear this kid tell me her mom was waiting for her in the car. That last night was all a bad dream.

She gazed up at me. "Naw . . . she's away."

"Away?"

"She split early this morning."

"What?" I asked in disbelief.

She beheld me suspiciously. "What's it to you?"

"Well . . . I-I . . ." I stumbled on my words until I thought of something to say. "She wanted me to come out and look at her VCR today. She said she was having some trouble." Then I pushed down my sunglasses and eyed her over the top of the frames. "Did you notice any problems while watching your tape?"

She shook her head. "I stayed over at my girlfriend's house last night."

"Oh." I looked across the street and then said, "Your mother went away then."

"Yeah."

"So I guess I won't be coming out to your house today."

She shrugged. "It was kinda sudden."

"Did she stop by your friend's house to tell you?" I inquired.

"No, she left me a note." She related.

"A note?" Since when did dead people write notes? She nodded.

"She didn't say anything about me fixing the machine?"

"Nope."

"Nice of her to let me know . . . I mean, I'm glad I didn't make that trip out there for nothing." I expressed displeasingly.

"I'm sorry." She said. "It was kinda sudden."

"Was there an emergency . . . a sick relative or something?" I kept pursuing the matter.

"Gee, you sure ask a lot of questions, Mister."

"Mitch. The name's Jeff Mitchum. Friends call me Mitch."

"I know." She replied casually.

"You think I should go to your house and fix the machine anyway?"

"You seem pretty concerned about my mother's machine?" She squinted up at me.

"Just wondering." I said, eyeing my store. "I don't have anything else to do today. My shop's a mess."

"You closing down the place?" She asked distressingly.

"Just until I get it repaired."

She seemed disappointed. "Too bad . . . you have the best selection in town."

"Do I?"

"Uh-huh."

"Tell you what, just for you, I'll keep renting you tapes. Free of charge." I proposed.

"How come?"

"Because I'm a swell guy." I smiled.

She didn't seem to buy my generosity. "Give me a break, pal."

"What kind of talk is that?" I laughed at her cynicism.

"I mean, *no*body gives anything away for zip." She asserted.

I nodded. "How old are you?"

"Seventeen."

I smirked. "The hell you are."

"Okay—sixteen."

"Your mother told me you were fifteen." I divulged.

She puckered her lips. "What's this thing you got going with my old lady?"

"HA!" I liked her nerve. "You're something else, kid."

"The name's Chloe."

"Pretty name."

"Yuck."

"No like?"

"It sucks." She griped. "Friends call me Chuck."

"Chuck. I like it."

"You want this tape back?" She held up the black plastic case.

"Sure." I shrugged.

"Here." She handed it to me. "I gotta split." She turned and started to walk away.

"What about your mom's VCR?" I inquired after her.

She halted, her back to me. "What about it?"

"I think your mom would have wanted me to look it over."

She put her hands on her hips and twisted around. "Enough already with the fuckin' machine!"

6

JAIL BAIT

WE DROVE TO HER HOUSE

in my Porsche. She sat next to me with her feet up on the dashboard. She was wearing blue plastic sandals, no socks, her toenails painted in fluorescent blue. I turned to look at her smooth, model-perfect cheekboned face. I felt foolish for ever thinking that she was a male. She had on Day-Glo lipstick and eye shadow. She was too pretty to be wearing so much make-up.

"You should try keeping your eyes on the road, Mitch." She said as she gazed straight ahead of her.

I laughed and focused on the blacktop. We were travelling along Three Mile Harbor Road to her home in Springs.

"You're a pretty young lady, Chuck." I commented, sounding like an old fart.

She rolled her eyes and sighed.

"Have many boyfriends?" I asked.

"Most of the boys out here are just that—boys." She wrinkled her nose.

"Like the older type do yah?"

"Sort of." She said with a shrug of her shoulder.

I beamed.

"College-aged, not ancient." She burst my bubble.

"I got the message." I was trying my best to keep cool, but I was very anxious to get to her place. I just had to see Nicola's bedroom again. If the body wasn't there, where was it? And who had moved it? "Been out here long?"

"A few years. Used to live on Fifth Avenue and come out here in the summer. Then my old lady got sick of the city or something. I think she was really worried about me. The schools and shit. My dad still stays in the apartment during the week, comes out on weekends."

"You like it out here?" I wondered.

"It's one big yawn, you know what I mean? Summers are okay, but during the winter—forget about it. Dullsville." She yawned dramatically.

"Yeah, gets bone-cold out here." I shivered from the thought.

"And the night life sucks." She hissed.

I smirked. "The night life? Aren't you a little too young . . ."

"Too young? Where do you come from, pops?" She hit me with glaring eyes.

"Guess I'm not too hip, huh?" I went along with her.

"I'll say. I may be only pushing sixteen but I've been around."

"Yeah, I can see that." I smiled to myself.

"You're new out here, right?"

"Just a year and a half. Used to come out here when I was a kid. Two weeks in the summer."

"Your folks had bread?" She asked incredulously.

"Nope." I said. "We used to rent a small cottage and go fishing. This place didn't look anything like this twenty, twenty-five years ago."

"I hear you were a cop—that right?"

"Gee, there're no secrets in this town."

"Why the hell would anyone want to be a dumb cop?" She asked directly.

"Must've been dumb." I shrugged.

"I'll say." She added.

I hung a right and drove up her driveway.

"How did you know how to get here?" She asked.

"I know this area well."

I pulled up in front of her house and shut off the engine. I caught her looking at me with suspicion.

"Really." I smirked.

"I'm wondering about you, Mitch." She cocked her head to one side.

"Oh?"

"Yeah . . ." She opened the door and ran ahead to the front door.

I hopped out and hurried after her. The house appeared quiet. It was a huge split-level on spacious, manicured grounds. Big Bucks in this neck of the woods. It looked different in the daylight. It was like I had never been there before.

A servant opened the door. She was a dark-haired woman in her mid-forties. I wondered where she had been last night.

"Janet, this is Mr. Mitchum, he's here to fix mom's VCR." Chloe said as she whipped by the uniformed woman.

I nodded. "Good afternoon."

The servant gave me the eye. I followed Chloe to her mother's bedroom.

She was standing by the machine, her hand on her hip. "Here you go."

I gave the place a quick once-over. It was spotless. A pungent disinfectant smell was in the air.

"Well, let's see." I began fussing with the machine.

"You need any help?" Chloe offered.

"No, I don't think so."

"Good, I want to take a quick dip—too muggy out." She walked towards the door pulling her shirt off on the way. She turned around and faced me, her small budding breasts exposed. "You want a cold drink?"

I swallowed hard and averted my eyes. Like mother, like daughter. "No . . . no thanks."

She shrugged and exited the room.

I waited a few minutes then went to the bed. The white fur cover was on it. I pulled it aside. The silver satin sheets had been replaced with blue ones. I took a deep breath and tore the sheet off the edge of the bed. A miraculous white mattress cover was beneath. It felt starchily new. I peeled that away and finally found the mattress. It appeared wet in spots. I found some dark red stains that somebody had tried to wash out. *Blood*. I remade the bed quickly then returned to the machine. I didn't know what to think now. If somebody was trying to frame me for murder why would they dispose of the body and clean up the mess? It just didn't make any sense.

I left the room and tried to find Chloe. I ran into the maid in the kitchen.

She gave me that dirty look again.

"Where's Chuck . . . Chloe?" I asked Old Iron-sides.

"Out back." She motioned with a flick of her thumb.

"Are her parents at home?"

She shook her head.

"I'm curious . . . are you a live-in servant?" I asked the stone-faced maid.

"I don't see how that's any of your business, Mr. Mitchum." She snapped offensively.

"Well, I've been looking for a maid . . . can't seem to find the right one. You seem very *thorough*." I winked.

She cocked her head to one side and burned me with her piercing brown eyes. "I work for the Gages on a full-time basis."

"Then you're a live-in?"

"No, Mr. Mitchum, I'm not." She huffed, obviously annoyed by my inquiry.

"Well, that's too bad about you being a full-time employee of this household. I could've really used somebody like you . . . especially last night. Jesus," I shook my head, "what a mess I made."

She straightened up and left the room in a huff.

Nice friendly type.

I went out back and caught Chloe, stark naked, posed on the diving board. She possessed a lithe, athletic body. She made a graceful dive into the kidney-shaped pool. She broke surface a few moments later and smiled at me. I came by the pool and squatted down. I tested the temperature of the water. It was cool and inviting.

"Come on in!" She offered.

"Didn't bring my trunks."

"So?" She swam up to me. She gripped the edge of the pool and stretched out, her moon-white buttocks breaking the surface.

"*Soooo*." I splashed water in her face and stood up.

"Chicken shit, are we?" She teased me.

"I always thought of you as the quiet, shy type. That's why I figured you never came into my shop." I remarked.

"Well, I guess you figured wrong." She smirked.

"How come you never came in?"

"I liked looking in your window better." She revealed.

"You mean, you liked looking at *yourself* in my monitor."

She smiled. "Maybe."

"You're something else, kid." I was beginning to appreciate her wise-ass mouth.

"Did you fix my mother's precious machine?"

"Yep . . . just needed a head cleaning." I related. "You never told me where your mother went."

"Who cares?" She splashed water on me.

"Pretty weird of her just splittin' like that." I persisted.

"Not for my mother . . . does it all the time. She meets some young stud and runs off with him. It happens all the time." She explained nonchalantly.

"What about your dad?" I was wondering if she was feeding me a line.

"What about him?"

I raised my eyebrows.

"He doesn't care . . . he has his own young playthings.'' She swam to the ladder and climbed out. She walked slowly and immodestly towards me. I noticed she was a true redhead, top and bottom, just like her mom. I picked up the towel that was draped over the chaise lounge and handed it to her. She wiped her face and rubbed her hair with it then placed it over her shoulders.

I shook my head. ''Are you always so open around strangers?''

''I don't have any hang-ups.''

''What about Janet?'' I asked of the maid.

''She's a bitch.'' She shrugged.

''Yeah, I kinda got the drift.''

''Stuck up.'' She picked up her can of Diet Pepsi and took a sip. ''Are you married or something?''

''Or something.'' I winked.

She took me in with azure peepers. ''You're in pretty good shape for your age.''

I laughed. ''Yeah, for an old bastard like me.''

''Why don't you join me in the pool?'' She asked seductively.

''I'll take a rain check.'' I said. ''I have to get going.''

''So soon?'' She sounded genuinely disappointed.

''Yeah.''

''Well, you have to drive me back to town to pick up my car.'' She reminded me.

''I know.''

''Give me a few minutes.'' She walked off towards the house. I followed her long, shapely legs with my eyes. I shook my head for the umpteenth time. Jesus, was she a knock out. But there was no way I was going to take a shot. Besides being jail bait, the last time I had taken a nibble I ended up with a disappearing corpse and a big, fat mystery. "Tell me something." I cried after her.

She swung around, her white skin glaring in the sunlight. "Yeah?"

"How come you're so pale? I would think since you go skinny-dipping you would be bronze by now."

"I'm not into skin cancer." She said and went into the house.

I went around to the front of the house to my car. When I got there a gray Buick passed by on the road. It struck me because the car was moving so slowly and the driver looked familiar. He was wearing dark sunglasses and staring straight at me. Where had I seen that face before?

I ran it through my brain's computer banks and came up with that stranger who had been in my shop yesterday. That pain-in-the-ass who didn't own a VCR. Hey, wait a minute. That was a mighty suspicious number he had pulled off. I mean, when you deal with the public you come across some weird folk, but this guy took the door prize. I wondered if he was somehow involved in this whole thing. I had to give Adam Hayes a call. He could help me out with this one.

"Sorry I took so long." Chloe said from behind.

I turned around. She was now wearing pink short-shorts and a Hawaiian shirt opened to her belly-button. But it wasn't her outfit that startled me. It was her sunglasses. She was wearing Yoko Ono Porsche Design wraps.

It sent a chill down my spine.

7

IS IT DEAD
OR IS IT MEMOREX?

ADAM PULLED UP in my driveway. I was leaning against the back of my car waiting for him. He looked like he'd gained twenty pounds since the last time I saw him. I smiled at him. He struggled out of the car. He leaned heavily on the opened door, taking his shades off and rubbing his eyes. He gazed at me with his fluid eyes then gave my property the once over. All this without uttering a word.

"How yah doin', Adam?" I remained where I was, my arms folded.

He nodded and began to walk towards me. He halted when he got to me, his brow beaded with sweat. He was so close I could smell the onions on his breath. Adam loved fried onion sandwiches.

"Nice spread, kid." He said in his breathy voice.

"I'm comfortable." I replied.

He finally showed his teeth as he eased into a smile. "Bet you are, Mitch, bet you are."

"I'm glad you could make it out."

"You sounded pretty desperate over the phone."

55

"Yeah, I guess I did." I put my arm around him.
"Come on—I'll show you how the other half live."

He eyed my Porsche. "Glad to see that you didn't
let it go to your head."

"You mean the car—it's ten years old—a relic,
for chrissakes."

"I mean *every*thing, man."

We walked through the gate and onto my grounds.
I brought him around the one-bedroom pool house
where I installed a gym, and showed off my circular
black-lined pool.

"Nice." He remarked in a monotone. He put his
sunglasses back on and hitched up his pants. "But I
didn't come all the way out here for a fuckin' tour."

"I'm sorry, Adam." I shrugged. "It's just been a
long time."

"Trying to ease back into it?" He asked.

"Something like that. I did invite you and Roxy
out a while back." I reminded him.

"That you did, Mitch." He acknowledged.

I looked him straight in the eye and asked, "You
still sore at me, Adam?"

"Naw." He put his hands on his hips and faced
me, his eyes hidden behind his dark shades. "You
weren't *that* good, Mitchum."

I smiled. "Fuck you, pal."

He pushed his head back and roared. "Ah, Mitch,
I guess I do miss yah."

"Funny way of showing it."

He gave me a bear-hug. "I could do with a brew."

"Coming right up."

We went into the main house and I took out a
couple of bottles of Amstel Light from the fridge.

We went into the media room and sat down on the sofa.

"I'm really impressed, Mitch." Adam took a pull from his beer. "Now this is living."

"It just took winning the lottery, man." I quipped.

"Lucky bastard." He shook his head.

"Used to think so."

He took me in. "What the hell's up, Mitch?"

I let out a long sigh and shook my head. "Unfuckingbelievable."

"How's Jesse?" He inquired, wondering if my problems were personal.

"She's fine . . . she's in the city . . . I haven't even told her yet."

"You haven't told me either." He arched his eyebrows.

I took a sip of my beer and began my story. "Well, it all started with this redhead."

"Uh-huh." He said in an all-knowing tone.

"It's not what you think." I held my finger up to him.

"Sure . . . what kind of trouble has your dick led you into now?" He asked with a shit-eating grin.

"I have it on videotape."

"You mean like the movies?"

"Yep."

"Hardcore or softcore?" He joked.

"I wish I could laugh."

I picked up my remote control and turned on the television set and the VCR. I just played the final moments of the tape. He let out a yelp when he saw me, bare ass naked, in bed with Nicola.

"I don't believe this!" He was having a good time. "When does the good stuff start to happen?"

"That happened before this."

"Then rewind it, man!" He requested zealously.

"Look." I pointed to the screen.

The woman with the long black hair entered the picture. She stood by the bed and . . .

"Jesus." He leaned forward, whipping off his sunglasses, his eyes popping out of his head.

The tape ended.

He eyed me. "What the fuck was that?"

"You tell me."

"*Murder.*" He gasped.

"That's what I would call it." I mumbled.

He gave me a sideway glance. "An ice pick?"

"Where've we seen that before?" I asked sarcastically.

"Who's the chick with the ice chopper?"

"I don't know . . . I don't even know why."

"Where's the body?" He wondered.

"Gone."

"WHAT?!" He asked in disbelief.

"Just disappeared . . . the place scrubbed down."

"I don't get it."

I threw my hands up. "You and me both, pal. Her daughter told me she left a note . . . went away on a trip."

"Got news for you—she ain't comin' back!" He retorted.

I reran the tape in slow motion for him.

Afterwards I said, "Tell me, is it *dead* or is it Memorex?"

"An ice pick." He repeated.

"Yeah, that's been eating me, too."

"Coincidence or did somebody do their homework on you?" Adam asked.

I shook my head. "Maybe if I knew the why."

"You mentioned something about your store?"

"Yeah, it was torched the same night."

He stood up and walked to the TV screen, the image of the killer frozen on it. "Not a very clear shot."

"She's disguised . . . and I have no straight-on shots of her." I clucked my tongue. "Thought she reminded me of you-know-who."

"Kate?" He asked.

"There's a resemblance."

"On *purpose*, y'think?" Adam was on the same wavelength as me.

"Maybe."

"You think the two incidents are related?"

"What else?"

"They hire the redhead to entertain you for the evening . . . keep you away from the shop." Adam ran it through his head.

"Sounds logical . . . but why kill her? And why *just* her? Who are they after?"

"Torch your shop and frame you for murder?" He inquired.

"But they disposed of the body for me!" I exclaimed.

"Just doesn't make sense." Adam shook his head again.

I raised my hands. "Now you know why I called you."

"You tell anyone else about this?"

"Not a soul."

"Her daughter—you said she got a note from her mom?"

"I didn't see it . . . she told me about it. She's fifteen. A real knockout like her mom."

"Nymphet City." He grinned ear-to-ear.

"Something like that and more." I accentuated.

"You dip into her, too?"

"Nope." I made a sour face.

"Is she giving you the straight dope?"

"I don't know." I hesitated. "She does own a pair of those sunglasses."

"The wraps?"

I acknowledged him.

"Owning the same brand of sunglasses doesn't make her a murderer." He said.

"I know . . . but it's something." I knew I was grabbing at straws.

"She and the old lady didn't get along?"

"I'm working on that angle . . . there was some tension between them."

"Enough to off her mother?" Adam wasn't buying it.

"I don't think so, but—"

"These rich suburban kids . . ."

"You got my drift."

"What do you want from me?" He asked me right out as was his style.

"Help." I replied.

"It's yours."

I shifted gears. "There is this other little thing . . . A guy came into my shop that very same day. I saw him again around the girl's home. A hood. An old-timer from Boston.''

"A mick?''

"Probably. You know the type.''

"A professional torch?'' He asked.

"Maybe a shooter.''

"Give me his description, I'll run him through the computer.'' Adam offered.

"I will.''

Just then the phone rang. I reached over and picked up the receiver. "Yeah?''

"Mitch?'' It was Jesse.

"Oh, hiya baby.''

"Where have you been . . . I've been calling for days.''

"I've been . . . preoccupied.''

"I've been worried sick about you, Mitch.'' She expressed passionately.

"I'm sorry, Jess, you see, there's been a fire.''

"A fire?!'' She screeched. "The house?''

"No, the shop . . . somebody torched it.''

"You're kidding?''

"It was arson.'' I related.

"Who would've done such a thing?'' She inquired.

"I don't know. I have Adam here. He's going to help me out.''

"You should've phoned me . . .''

"I told you . . . I've been preoccupied . . . the fire and all.''

"That's my Mitch, always keeping things to himself. You must really be upset.''

"I'll survive. I'd just like to find out why somebody wants to put me out of business.'' I said.

"I have to go. I'm on my break. Promise me you'll call tonight." She insisted.

"Of course. Love you." I hung up, then eyed Adam. "How am I going to explain all this to Jesse?"

"You mean without mentioning the dead redhead?" Adam asked.

"Yeah."

"Women." Adam shook his head. "You sure have had your problems with them."

"Tell me about it." I sighed.

8

NIGHT VISITOR

AFTER MAKING A BARBE-
CUE for Adam, I sent him home. It was near ten
and I knew his wife would be worried about him. It
had been good to see him again after all this time. We
had gone on for hours talking about the old days when I
was still on the force. I just wished our reunion had been
under better circumstances. Here I was with a murder
rap hanging over my head and lots of unanswered
questions. I was glad Adam would look into a few
things for me. Including a profile on Nicola and her
husband. I needed as much information as I could get
to figure this one out.

Then I remembered Jesse. I ought to call her. I
loaded the rest of the dishes into the dishwasher and
went into the media room to make the call.

It was then that I heard the splash.

It sounded like someone was taking a dip in my pool.

I headed out the back way, past my patio, and
around to the pool. The night spotlights were on and it
was all aglow. Inside was Chloe's trim form. She
surfaced at the edge and gave me a broad smile.

"How did you find me?"

"I asked around." She climbed out of the pool and stood before me in all her naked glory. Her pink nipples were standing on end in the crisp cool air.

"You're going to catch your death."

"The water's warm."

I shook my head and walked away. I heard her footsteps behind me as she followed me into the pool house. I went to the closet and pulled out a towel. I handed it to her.

She was still beaming as she wrapped the towel around her shoulders, her teeth chattering. She wandered over to my gym. She sat down on the weight bench. "You work out?"

"Guess so."

"You mad at me?" She asked.

"I don't like surprises." I complained.

"I would've called but I didn't have the number." She smiled demoniacally.

"I've had a long day." I sighed.

She eyed the bed. "This where you sleep?"

"It's for my guests."

"Aren't I a guest?"

"An uninvited one." I reminded her.

"Gee, you sound like you're on the rag." She said out of the corner of her mouth.

"Listen, kid, I'm tired. I had a bad night. I would like to hit the sack."

"So, who's stopping you?"

"You are." I said.

She cocked her head to the side. "I thought we were getting along pretty well today."

"Maybe you thought wrong."

"Okay." She stood up. "I got the message." She threw the towel at me and stormed past me.

I grabbed hold of her arm. "Where the hell are you going?"

"Get your hands off me!" She snarled.

Our eyes interlocked. She was fuming. I released my grip. "I'm sorry."

"Should be." She wiped her nose with the back of her hand. "I just felt lonely."

"You got friends."

"You call them *friends*?" She snapped.

"They're your own age."

She glared at me. "You sure have a hang-up about my age."

"You're a kid, Chuck. Face it." I said frankly.

"Nice guy."

"Why don't you get dressed? I'll give you a glass of milk and you can head home."

"Milk?" She asked with a grimace.

"Isn't that what kids drink?"

"Maybe back in prehistoric times when you were a kid." She retorted.

"I'm only in my thirties, for chrissakes."

"Is that all? I figured at least fifty." She said sarcastically.

"Rotten kid." I uttered as I headed out the door.

When I got out onto the patio the phone rang. I ran into the main house to answer it. I got it in the media room. Chloe was already on the line.

"Who's this?" I heard Jesse's voice ask.

"Chuck—who're you?"

"I got it, Chuck." I said. "Hello, Jesse."

"Who's Jesse?" Chloe asked. "You said you weren't married."

"Get off the phone, Chloe!" I demanded.

I heard a click. "I'm sorry Jesse, I was just about to call you."

"Who's this Chloe . . . Chuck—whatever her name is?"

"Some pain-in-the-ass kid."

"Kid?"

"That's right."

"What's she doing there at this time of night?" Jesse asked accusingly.

"I don't know . . . I never got a chance to ask her." I moaned.

"Jeffrey Mitchum are you up to no good?" Jesse asked scornfully.

"Cool it, Jesse. She's a kid. Fifteen years old. A brat. She's a customer. She came out to return a tape she rented. I told you they torched my shop."

"You're working out of the house now?" She asked.

"For a little while . . . until I clean up the store." I explained.

"You promised me, Mitch." She said in a threatening tone.

"Don't start that, Jesse. Please, I've been through enough." I sighed.

There was a long pause. "I'm sorry, Mitch, but sometimes . . . "

"I know . . . I know." I said. "When're you coming home?"

"Friday night . . . I can't swing it any sooner." She said. "I miss you, Mitch."

"Me too." I looked up when Chloe entered the room. She was wearing Calvin Klein briefs and athletic shirt. I wanted to hit her over the head for upsetting Jesse.

"What do you want to do this weekend?" Jesse asked.

I rolled my eyes. I was in the middle of a nightmare and she wanted to know how we were going to entertain ourselves this weekend. "How about if I make you a nice lobster dinner on Friday?"

"I'll be too pooped to enjoy it." She already sounded fatigued.

The agency was really working her hard between model shoots and television commercials.

Chloe yawned while she sat on a chair and began leafing through one of Jesse's magazines.

"Are you going to tell me what's been going on?" She asked.

"Yes, I'll tell you everything when you get back home. I can't talk about it over the phone. For all I know it might be bugged." I said.

"Bugged?"

"Somebody's after me, Jes." I said quietly, hoping Chloe won't hear me.

"Oh, Mitch!" Jesse exclaimed. "This sounds more serious than I thought. What's going on?"

I swallowed hard. "Jesse—not now. Not until I find out for myself, I have to play it safe. Understand?"

"Now I'm really worried about you, Mitch." Jesse said sincerely.

"I'll be fine. You know I can handle myself. I'll see you on Friday, okay? I love you, Jesse."

Chloe put her finger down her throat.

I sneered at her.

"I love you."

"See you on Friday."

"Good night."

I hung up.

Chloe flung the magazine down on the floor. "What kind of name is Jesse?"

"It sure beats the hell out of Chuck."

"Sounds like a real bitch to me." She said under her breath.

"You had no right to answer my phone, young lady." I scolded her.

"I was only doing you a favor."

"Some favor." I huffed.

"She always so high-strung?"

"Only when some fresh little tramp answers the phone!"

My reply hit her like a slap across the face. She looked down and sucked in her cheeks. She got up and walked out of the house.

I scanned the ceiling. "Jesus Christ!" I raked my fingers through my hair.

I decided to go after her.

I found her in the pool house. She was lying face-down on the bed sobbing away. I came into the room and sat down on the edge. Her body heaved with every loud sob. I put my hand on her shoulder. "Shhhh. I'm sorry, Chloe. I didn't mean what I said. I was angry. I had a right to be angry."

I just couldn't help thinking about her mother. Here was this poor kid who didn't know that her mother was never coming back. She would be doing a lot more crying soon.

"Come on, Chuck."

She turned around onto her back and rubbed her eyes. She suddenly appeared very young. She took her hands away and eyed me through her sore red orbs. "You know you're a real creep."

"Never said otherwise."

"Don't you know how to treat women?" She asked.

"I wonder sometimes."

"You could use some lessons."

"Have much experience with other men do yah?"

"I sure as hell never met anyone quite like you, creep."

I smiled. "Okay, I'm a creep. But you were wrong, Chloe."

"Chuck." She corrected me.

"Chuck."

"If you say so."

"You were."

"I didn't know your girlfriend was so sensitive."

"I didn't know you were so sensitive either."

"It wasn't nice what you said." She pouted.

"I apologized, didn't I?"

She managed a smile.

"You better get dressed and get on home."

"Can't I stay here with you?" She asked with a childlike voice.

"What about your family . . . aren't they worried about you?"

"I told you, my mom's away." She said disagreeably.

"What about your father?"

"He's in the city."

"Then who's minding you?" I wondered.

"Nobody—I don't need a baby sitter," she said defensively.

"I can't believe your folks would leave you by yourself."

She sat up. "Well, they did!"

I said softly, "You can't stay here, Chuck."

She stared into my eyes, our noses almost touching. "You have pretty green eyes . . . like a cat." She said as she poured on the charm. "Please let me stay."

I shook my head.

She wrapped her arms around me. "Please." I felt her lips against mine.

I pushed her away and stood up. "If you stay, you sleep in here."

Her lips curled into a grin. "And where are you going to sleep?"

"In my own bed . . . *alone* . . . inside the *locked* main house." I said as I stood over her.

She pulled off her shirt and lay back on the bed. That smile never leaving her face.

"Good night, Chuck."

She began to peel off her briefs.

I ran out and shut the door, locking it from the outside. I saw her come to the glass door, trying the handle. She stood there in her birthday suit, her breath fogging up the glass. "YOU CREEP!" She shouted as she battered the door.

I waited until she gave up, her body slinking against the door to the floor. She stood up, gave me the finger, and got into bed.

I said, "Pleasant dreams."

9

A NEW ANGLE

I WAS DREAMING about Kate again. But I no longer remembered her face. Instead, I saw her with the Porsche Design wraparound sunglasses and the yellow slicker . . .

And the ice pick.

I recalled the time I had confronted Bobby Finkelstein. It had been during the time of his investigation into Kate's murder. . . .

I could tell he wasn't getting anywhere by the despondent expression on his face. A short plump guy with big black bags under his eyes, he sat behind his desk eating a glazed donut and sipping lukewarm coffee from a cardboard cup. His thick mustache was flaked with sugar as he spoke with his mouth open. "I wish I could tell you more, man."

I didn't say anything but he still *heard* me.

"It's a real bitch of a case. No leads. No nuthin'. Just a lot of man hours . . . y'know what I mean?"

I nodded, still trying to keep my cool. I just didn't like this asshole. I thought he was a bad cop. Too lazy. He waited for everything to come to him instead of going out and breaking his ass.

"What 'bout you—did you dig up anything?"

I shook my head.

He sipped his coffee and made a face. "This is even worse than my old lady's gook. Shit." He wiped his mouth with a paper napkin. "I heard about that kid you worked over. I told you he wasn't our man."

I shrugged, still waiting for something constructive from this slob.

"Nasty business, Mitch. I could lock you up for that. I mean, if the kid wasn't a piece of shit anyway." He let out a deafening belch. "Excuse me."

I sighed. "Haven't you got anything, Bobby?"

"Hell no!" He couldn't look me in the eye. "But I did find this interesting." He handed me a dispatch from a downtown precinct. "Seems there's a guy running around down there that matches our MO. Break-ins, rapes. Uses a sharp instrument."

" 'A very thin dagger.' " I read aloud from the report. "MMMMM . . . might be something."

"Maybe." Finkelstein said. "But a dagger ain't an ice pick."

"An ice pick might look like a very thin dagger to some." I winked.

"But this dude isn't cutting anyone never mind killing them." He conveyed.

"Maybe Kate resisted . . . he didn't have any options."

"Come on, Mitch, Kate looked like she was asleep when it happened. Thank God for that." Finkelstein added.

I stood up. "At least it's something."

He stabbed his fat thumb at me. "It's nothing! Zippo, Mitch. And it's out of my jurisdiction."

"Not *mine*." I sneered. . . .

I heard a noise in my dream that stirred me. I wanted so hard to wake up and forget all these bad memories.

I woke up after nine to a dark gray morning. A brisk wind rattled the shutters. It was the kind of day to remain in bed, covers drawn over head. But I remembered I had locked Chloe in the pool house and it would be cruel to keep her captive much longer. Though the thought brought a smile to my face. I stood up and stretched my limbs, my bones crackling like a roaring fire. I hadn't worked out all week and my muscles were stiffening. I took a quick shower and slipped into my briefs and a cotton robe. I went downstairs and prepared the coffee before going out to the pool house.

The wind ruffled the trees, a storm brewing in the cloudy sky. She was waiting for me in her Calvin Klein underwear at the glass door, hand impatiently on hip. She looked like one of Calvin's magazine spreads come to life. I unlocked the door and she pushed it open. She brushed by me as she hurried into the main house. I trailed after her, finding her sitting on the kitchen cabinet, her crossed legs dangling beneath her. The palms of her hands flat on the Formica counter top, her back arched, head cocked, a penetrating gaze.

She said, "Mornin' creep."

I said, "Sleep well?"

"Yes—considering."

The coffee maker belched and stewed noisily in the background.

"Looks like rain." I remarked as I took out a package of English muffins.

"Nice day to stay in bed." She smirked.

I took her in. I was growing tired of her bitch in heat number. Maybe I should try a different defensive tactic. I came up to her and smiled. I undid my robe and put my hands on my hips. She looked down at me. "What did you have in mind?" I asked.

She said, "I thought only fags wore bikini briefs."

I glanced down at my blue Jockeys. "Jim Palmer isn't a fag."

"Who's Jim Palmer?"

"Never mind. Besides, what's a girl doing wearing men's cotton briefs?"

"All the girls are wearing these."

I crinkled my nose. "It doesn't do much for me."

She jumped down off the counter and sat down at the table. I closed my robe. Must've scared her off.

"I like bacon and scrambled eggs." She put in her order.

"Do I look like a short-order cook to you?" I asked.

"You have any orange juice?"

"In the fridge."

She sighed and got up and poured herself a glass. She took it back to the table and sat down again.

"Thanks for pouring me one." I said sarcastically.

She drank down hers and giggled.

I started to make her breakfast. "What do you plan on doing with your life?" I eyed her. "What about college?"

"I never thought about it."

"How come?"

"My father will decide." She stated.

"He do all the thinking for you?" I asked, a bit disturbed by her answer.

"Don't all fathers?" She retorted in a singsong tone.

"Mine didn't." I said. "What does your father do?"

"He's in video."

"Say what?" I snapped out of my morning grogginess.

"He works at RayBeam Video."

"RayBeam?"

"Yep. He's the president or something."

"I thought that renegade director, whatshisface—Sam Rayburn, owns that company?"

"He does. He owns it, my dad runs it."

"Ummmm . . . your mother never mentioned that to me." I conveyed aloud as I drifted off in deep thought.

She gave me a dirty look. "Did you make it with my mom?"

I laughed. "Of course not."

"You sure talk a lot about her." She declared distastefully.

"She's an attractive lady."

"I'm prettier." She proclaimed, a tinge of jealousy in her voice.

"In your own way."

"She's got big tits and hips." She carried on.

"I'll say." I remarked gleefully.

"I was thinking about going into modeling."

"Yeah, you're skinny enough."

"Whaddaya mean by skinny?"

I put her plate in front of her. "You know, slinky."

She huffed and wolfed down her breakfast.

I sat down adjacent from her and sipped my coffee. "Slow down."

"Now you sound like my mother." She whined.

"Not your dad?"

"I don't get to see him much . . . and when I do he's always nice to me."

"He buy you things?"

"Uh-huh."

"Did he buy you that 300 ZX?" I inquired.

"For my sixteenth birthday."

"But you're only fifteen . . . hey, how can you have a driver's license at your age?"

"Who needs a license?"

"Does your dad know you're driving around without a license?" I was sounding more and more like an old fart.

She shrugged. "The car arrived two months earlier than he expected . . . what does he expect me to do just let it sit there on the driveway?"

I shook my head. "Nice life."

"It's okay."

"But you're bored."

"Who isn't?"

"Me, for one."

"Believe me, you may not be bored, but you're boring." She managed to get in another dig.

"Thank you."

"Tell me about your girlfriend."

"Jesse?"

She laughed at her name. "Yeah, Jesse."

"She's an actress."

"Oh yeah?" Her ears perked up.

"And a model."

"Do I know her?"

"You've seen her."

"Is she pretty?"

"Very."

"But she's a witch."

"No, she isn't."

"Then why aren't you two married?" She continued to pump me.

"Someday perhaps." I stated.

She finished her breakfast and pushed her plate away.

"You better be going." I announced.

"Are you trying to get rid of me?" She asked odiously.

"Yes."

"Creep." She got up and stood by me. "You don't like me much, huh?"

"I wouldn't say that."

"Then how come you're always trying to get rid of me?" She seemed sincerely hurt.

"I have things to do, Chuck."

"You think I'm just a kid, right?"

I thought it over for a second. "Right."

"I guess you have a hang-up."

"You already told me that last night." I reminded her.

She leaned over and kissed me on the forehead. "Maybe someday you'll get over it."

"Maybe." I smiled.

She went to the door. "Thanks for breakfast."

"Sure."

She went out to the pool house.

I sat there and kicked around the information she had given me about her father. RayBeam Video. I had some of their titles. They did mostly offbeat fare including a hardcore pornographic line.

Then it hit me.

Hardcore porn.

X-TRATERRESTRIAL. It was a porno title RayBeam put out. *E.T.* with sex featuring porn goddess Zoe Savage. A few months ago I had sold a copy to a regular customer. He had returned it the next day with a major complaint. It wasn't X-TERRESTRIAL but the real *E.T.*. I had given him another tape and the next time the salesman showed up, I complained. I had put the tape aside and hadn't thought about it since. But now it struck me as being fishy. Come to think of it, I hadn't seen the RayBeam salesman ever since. He used to come by every month with a sample case filled with the latest RayBeam releases, mostly porno. I've since begun buying my porno from another source and ordering specific RayBeam titles by mail. I wondered if he knew more about the *E.T.* tape than he let on. His name was Victor Wesen, like the oil.

He was a big guy, well over six feet tall and carried himself well. I used to look forward to his visits. He had a great sense of humor. But that day when I told him about the tape mix up, he became quite concerned.

"I'm really sorry about that." He declared, raking his fingers through his shaggy salt-and-pepper hair.

Pushing sixty, he was as solid as a rock. "Where is this tape?"

I shrugged. "Around somewhere."

"Let me get a credit for you on it. Do you know where it is?"

"Around." I scanned the store briefly. "Maybe back at the house."

"Well, I'm going to need that tape to credit your account."

"Hey, man, aren't I good for it?"

"Of course." He laughed.

"I mean, I'm not bullshittin' you."

"I know that. But my boss doesn't know you from a hole-in-the-wall."

"I don't know where the fuck it is—I'll mail it to your company."

"No." He shook his head while he held up his hands. "Don't do *that*."

"Hey, what's with you?"

He smiled uneasily. "Nothing . . . I'm . . . I'm not having a great day." He took out a handkerchief and began wiping the sweat that was beading up on his forehead.

"Are you okay . . . are you ill?" I helped him to a chair.

He sat down and started to laugh. "I'm great . . . never felt better."

I thought he was acting very strangely. He was so different from his usual jovial self.

He put his case on his lap. "I got some good stuff for you this month."

"Oh, yeah?"

"I have this new one—*HOT WET NURSES*." He

pulled out a four color brochure. "A lot of naked pregos and lactating mothers in this one!"

I squirmed up my face. "Sounds a little extreme for these parts. I need more gay shit. The boys of summer really go for that stuff."

"How about *LONGER AND HARDER*?" He offered.

"Sounds more like it." I glanced through the order form. I noticed that his hands were shaking. "Come on, Vic, what gives here—you're a fucking wreck."

He stood up and took back his brochure. "I-I-I have to get back . . ." He ran to the door. "I'll be back!" He vanished.

When I hadn't heard from him again, I decided to mail off a grievance to RayBeam about the *E.T.* screw-up. They had sent me back a form letter saying they fouled up during duplication.

But it all seemed so strange to me. First off, *E.T.* was not available on video tape as of this time. Secondly, surely RayBeam would not be releasing it on their label. That was a major Hollywood blockbuster, no way would it appear under the RayBeam label. It hadn't sunk in at the time. What the hell did I know? I was pretty green in the business. But now with Chloe's dad being a RayBeam executive and my shop being burned it could only mean one thing . . . *videotape piracy*.

At least it was something to start with. They had torched my shop to destroy the evidence—the tape itself. Of course, it didn't explain Nicola's murder. How the hell was that related?

I stood up. Now what did I do with that tape? I went into the media room and scanned my collection.

There it was. I pulled it off the shelf and felt relieved. At least they didn't get it.

I heard a car being started on my driveway.

Chloe.

I should ask her more questions about her father. I ran out the front door to the driveway. She was already backing out onto the street. I yelled out. She just waved and took off.

"Shit."

Then I saw the gray Buick follow after her. It was him again. I ran down to the street and memorized his license plate number just before he made his turn onto 27. They were New York rental plates. I hurried back into the house and wrote it down. I would call Adam and have him run it through the Department of Motor Vehicles.

Now the fog was lifting. I had something to follow through on. My cop instincts were returning.

I went up to my bedroom to get dressed. I opened the bottom drawer of my dresser and pulled out a case. I opened it. Inside rested my Walther Model P 38 K nine millimeter pistol. I picked up the snubbed weapon. Adam had always given me hell about using this gun. It hadn't been issued by the department. But I had preferred its compactness for my undercover duty. I popped in an eight-round cartridge. Since murder was already in the picture, I had to be prepared for anything. There was a lot I didn't know about. Video piracy might just be the tip of the iceberg.

If they were playing for keeps, so was I.

10

DRIVE, HE SAID

I FILLED ADAM IN on the latest
information. He still had nothing for me. He suggested I talk to Chloe again. Get as much dope as I
could on her father. He agreed that they were probably after that video tape. But there must have been
more to it. There was no reason to take Nicola out if
they were only involved with video tape piracy. I
decided to drive out to Chloe's place.

Her shiny new car was parked in the driveway
when I pulled up. I didn't notice the gray Buick
lurking anywhere nearby. I went up to the front door
and rang the bell. I heard the musical chimes faintly
behind the door.

Janet opened the door and glared at me with her
dark eyes.

"I'm here to see Chloe."

"She's not home."

I cocked my head to one side, taking in this witch
of a woman. "Her car's parked on the driveway."

She craned her head over my shoulder to peek out.
"Yes, it is."

"What did she do—*walk*?"

She pushed her head back defensively and announced, "She's not at home, Mr. Mitchum."

I put my hand on my hip and sighed. "Listen, Janet, I really have to see her. It's important."

"Well, she's not here."

"Then I'll wait for her to come home." I threatened.

"That won't be possible."

"Why's that?"

"She will be gone for quite some time." She stepped back to close the door. "Goodbye."

I put my foot against the door and shoved my way in. "Listen, lady, I said I have to see her!"

"You're very rude." She snapped.

"Where is she?" I asked assertively.

"She's gone."

I ground my teeth, having difficulty controlling my temper. "WHERE?"

"To the city." She replied.

"The *city*?"

"Yes."

"When will she be back?"

"I don't know."

"Take a guess." I suggested odiously.

"A week, maybe longer . . ."

"WHAT?" I asked inconceivably.

"Her father came home to collect her."

"Where in the city?"

"Mr. Gage's apartment.™

"The address!" I demanded.

"That's none of your business!" She retorted viciously.

"She has a tape of mine. She has to return it or I'll charge her for it."

"I'm sure Mr. Gage can afford it."

I saw I wasn't getting anywhere with this one. "Let me understand this now. Mr. Gage came home and took her with him to his apartment in the city?"

"That's correct."

"Just like that." I snapped my fingers. "Without warning. She packed her bags—"

"*I* packed them this morning while she was . . . was out." She beheld me disapprovingly.

"She didn't know about it then?"

That old gray face managed to smile. "No, she wasn't too happy about it at all . . ." She caught herself and sobered up. "I don't know why I'm telling you this."

I reached into my pocket and pulled out a wad of bills. "I'll make it worth your while, Janet."

"If you don't leave this instant, Mr. Mitchum, I'm calling the police. There are laws against people like you. She's only a child . . ." She threatened.

"I didn't lay a hand on her." I conveyed.

She held her stance dauntlessly.

"I need the address."

She wouldn't budge.

"Okay." I turned on my heels and went to my car. I heard the door slam loudly behind me. I slid into the seat and started the engine. Then I saw the gray Buick in the rear view mirror pull up behind me. I shut off the engine. He got out of his car and swaggered over. He stood by my door, staring straight ahead.

"You've been seeing too much of the girl, Mitchum."

"What are you her keeper?" I looked up at him.

He snickered, shifting his weight from one foot to the other. "Something like that."

"You buy that VCR yet?"

He broke into a toothy grin. "No, not yet. I don't like those newfangled contraptions." He still would not look at me.

"We never have been formally introduced."

He shook his ugly head. "Nope."

"Seems you know my name but I don't know yours."

"Seems like it." He replied.

"Could you tell me what the hell's going on?"

"Haven't you figured it out yet, Mitchum?" He asked, adding fervently, "Weren't you a cop?"

"I don't have the time to play games with you, asshole." I started to open my door. That was when he swung around and held my door shut with his foot. I was looking up the bluish black barrel of a .45 automatic.

"Temper . . . temper." He spoke sweetly. "I'll blow that pretty face of yours away if you misbehave." He continued in his patronizing tone. "Now— you have something I want."

"What would that be?"

He bared his teeth again. "Don't fuck with me."

"You're not about to blow me away in broad daylight, *schmuck*."

"Try me." He said with a sinister grin.

"You'll never get what you're after if you whack me."

He straightened up. "That's why we're going to take a little ride to your place. Isn't that where you're hiding it?"

"Maybe."

"It's not in your shop." He related.

"Didn't do a very thorough job of torching it."

He shrugged. "Maybe I'll have better luck taking care of you."

"Like the way you handled Nicola Gage?"

"I didn't like cleaning up after you, Mitchum. What kind of sick mind would do that to such a pretty lady?" He asked repugnantly.

"You tell me, pal. Who did you use to pull that number off?"

He beheld me confoundedly. "Nobody there but you and her, Mitchum, whaddaya tryin' to feed me?"

"You think *I* did it?" I asked incredulously.

"Nobody else but."

"You mean it wasn't—"

"I'm in a hurry!" He cut me off. "Let's go—my car."

I got out of my car and walked back to his. He frisked me ineptly, missing my ankle holster. "You drive." He tossed me the keys.

I went behind the wheel and started the engine. He slid in next to me, the gun pressed against my ribs.

"Where to?" I asked.

"The tape." He replied.

"What tape?"

He nudged me with the pistol. A sharp pain swept across my side. I coiled my head around to face him, pressure swelling inside me. "You do that one more time . . ."

He did it again.

I whimpered. My eyes welled up with tears. I sucked in a heavy dose of air. Exhaled slowly. Slowly. Trying to retain my composure. ''You're dead, man.'' I managed to choke out before he shoved the gun into my ribs again and again.

''DRIVE!'' He commanded.

I backed out onto the street and headed towards Three Mile Harbor Road.

''All this for a fucking tape?'' I inquired.

''Shut up!'' He shouted.

''I had forgotten all about it until you came around.''

''Gage can't afford any loose ends.'' He disclosed.

''Does that mean you don't want just the tape? Huh? Does that mean you have to silence me?'' I hung a left onto Three Mile Harbor Road.

''That wasn't in the deal.'' He mumbled.

''What deal?''

''I was hired to destroy the tape—period.'' He said unequivocally.

''What about Gage's wife?''

''Nothing seems to have worked out like the original plan.'' He shook his head in disgust.

''Was murder in the original plan?''

He focused on me. ''Of course not.''

''That means you're getting deeper and deeper into this. Arson is one thing. But murder? You're playing in the big leagues now, pal.''

''Didn't I tell you to shut up?''

''I have friends on the force . . . I can help you.'' I persisted.

''No way.'' He replied.

''We can make a deal.'' I would not relent.

"I don't make deals with dead men." He declared.

"I'm not dead."

"Sure you are . . . you just don't know it yet." The fiendish smile reappeared.

I stopped at the red light at the intersection of Main and Newtown. I faced him. "The police station is right over there. What do you say?"

"What do you take me for, Mitchum? I told you—no deals. I don't deal with cops. I don't like cops. Even ex-cops. Get it?"

"You prefer prison life?"

"It ain't so bad." He admitted candidly.

"Spend a lot of time there?" I inquired.

"On and off." He boasted.

"For playing with matches?"

"One stretch for that."

"Nothing more serious?"

"The light's green."

I drove on. "I would do some heavy thinking if I were you."

"I would do some heavy praying if I were you." He cackled.

"At least fill me in . . . what's Gage up to?"

He nudged me again. "I'm tired of talking."

I pulled off the main road and onto my dirt road. The few residents in our area wanted to keep as many tourists away from our neck of the woods as possible so we didn't pave the road. I turned into my driveway and shut off the engine.

"Now let's be smart about this, Mitchum." He glared at me through slits.

I opened the door and put my feet on the ground. I heard him open his door and slide across the seat.

That was when I reached into my ankle holster and came up with my Walther. ''FREEZE!'' My arms were stretched across the top of the car, the pistol clutched in my right hand, my left hand supporting my wrist.

I caught him off-guard. He waited a few beats to make up his mind.

''DROP IT!'' I ordered.

He hesitated.

''COME ON!'' I growled.

He dropped his gun and raised his hands.

''Walk away from the car. Over there.''

He backed up the driveway.

''OKAY!'' I came up to him, my gun in hand. ''Now it's my turn.'' I whipped him across the face with my pistol. His head sprang back with a spray of blood gushing from his mouth. He fell onto the ground and landed flat on his back. He sat up in a stupor and wiped the blood with the back of his hand.

I held my sore ribs and smiled. ''Now we have an understanding. Right?''

He nodded.

''First off—what's your name?''

''Pike.'' He said painfully.

''What's coming down, Pike?'' I inquired.

''All I want is the tape.'' He uttered.

''Gage hired you to get it.''

He acknowledged me.

''What else?''

''That's it.''

''There's more to it than that.'' I insisted.

''That's all I was hired to do.'' He maintained.

"To locate the tape and destroy it?"

"That's right."

"What about Nicola's body?"

"That was . . ." He paused.

"Go on."

"I ain't saying no more." He stated unswervingly.

"Don't get me mad again, Pike!" I threatened.

"Go ahead . . . pull the trigger." He waved his hand at me dauntlessly.

"Don't push me, Pike."

"I said too much already. I won't say another thing without my lawyer." He sneered.

I came closer to him and squatted down. "You don't seem to understand, Pike. I'm not a cop anymore. I don't have to play by the rules." I smiled. "Get that through your thick skull."

Now he smiled. "You ain't about to shoot me, Mitchum."

"Who said anything about shooting you, Pike?" I pressed the nose of my gun against his sore lip.

He flinched and pulled away.

"Getting the picture now, pal?"

Our eyes interlocked. I wondered how far I would have to go to break through to this turkey. He wouldn't care if I remade his face. It could only improve it. He probably had a high pain tolerance after his time in the ring.

"You were a human punching bag, right?" I asked.

He remained silent. I just heard his heavy Darth Vader breathing.

"Golden Gloves? Pro?" I persisted.

"In the Navy." He conveyed.

"Any good?"

He snickered.

Enough of this small talk. "Well, where do we go from here, Pike?"

I didn't even see it coming. A big fat fist seemed to come out of nowhere. BOOM. I saw a rainbow of colors then just blackness.

He was good alright. *Real* good.

11

BAD DREAMS

I WAS IN DREAMLAND for hours. When I opened my eyes, I found myself in Nicola's bed. The television set was on, my image on the screen. I watched myself on TV. I was wearing a yellow slicker, a long black-haired wig, and the Porsche sun shields. I was creeping around the bed. A woman was lying there, her back to the camera. I raised the ice pick that I had clenched in my fist. Just when I was about to strike, the woman turned around to face me. It was Kate. She let out a scream that stirred me from my nightmare. . . .

I opened my eyes again . . . but this time it was for real. I felt cold and wet. The sky was gray and cloudy, a steady stream of rain falling. I sat up. I was drenched. My jaw was sore. I struggled to my feet. The driveway was empty. I staggered to the house. I went through the front door and into the media room. As I suspected, it was a shambles. My tapes were spilled all over the floor. I didn't bother to look. I knew he hadn't found it. Did he really think I was that stupid? I went into the bathroom and began to peel off my clothes. I glanced into the mirror. My lip was swollen and caked with black dried blood. My right side looked like one gigantic black-and-blue mark. It even hurt to breathe.

I wondered why Pike didn't wake me after he couldn't find the tape. Unless he had figured out where I kept it.

I took a shower and got dressed. It was just after six when I finished. I called for a cab. I would have him take me to my car back at Chloe's place.

While I waited I packed a small bag. I planned on driving into the city tonight. I was impatient to meet Gage. I owed him one. And then some.

In order to get to Gage, I had to track down Wesen, the video tape salesman. He might be useful to me. He obviously knew the score and that was why he had split so suddenly. Perhaps he had been afraid of my blowing the whistle on them after I received the pirated *E.T.* tape.

The taxi service showed up and drove me to my car. He tried to start some small talk. I didn't oblige him. I wasn't in the mood for talking. Besides, my jaw was hurting. And my ribs. The only thing I wanted to do was meet up with my dear friend Mr. Pike. I wondered if his jaw was giving him some trouble too. I reached down and felt for my Walther. It was tucked away on my ankle. Next time I ran into Pike he was going to hear my Walther speak.

The cab dropped me off before the house. My car was in the driveway. I paid him and he drove off. I went over to the car and got behind the wheel. I put my hand under the seat and pulled out two video tapes. One was the tape Pike was looking for, the other was the one with Nicola's murder on it. I put them back, started the engine, and backed out of the driveway. I gazed at the house and saw someone at one of the front windows looking at me from behind the drapes. Probably Janet, the dragon lady. I shifted gears and burned rubber as I took off down the road.

That bad dream I had while I had been unconscious bummed me out. Ever since all this happened I couldn't get Kate out of my head. I'd been trying to forget about it for two years now. But it kept coming back like old syndicated reruns. Nothing ever dies.

I flashed back to that night. After I had checked out her ransacked apartment, I went down to the morgue with Adam. I just had to see her body. I wanted to make sure she was really dead.

"Why are you doing this to yourself?" Adam asked as we drove downtown.

"Because." I replied.

"I told you her parents identified the body."

I faced him. He was behind the wheel of the unmarked Ford. He drove with his hands in his lap, two fingers gripping the steering wheel at six o'clock. The Fat Man's way of driving. I said, "I have to see her."

He shook his head as he let loose some steam. "Man-oh-man, you like beating on yourself. She's gone, Mitch. There's nothing to see but a corpse."

"Did I ever tell you why I split with her, Adam?"

He stopped for a red light. "I thought she split with you?"

I shrugged. "She split . . . I split . . . it takes two, man."

"Take it easy . . ."

"I still love . . . *loved* her, y'know. We were married for seven years for chrissakes. Good years . . ." I paused to correct myself. "Mostly bad years."

"A cop's life." Adam asserted. "We've all been through it, Mitch. I'm on my second marriage now. So far, so good. But you never know. Things change. People change. Not much you can do about it. It's a good idea for you to get the hell out of this life. Start fresh. Bread's not a problem now. Run off with Jesse to a fuckin' deserted island or somethin'. Yeah, I think you got the right idea, Mitch."

"Maybe." I mumbled.

He faced me. "Go on with your plans, man, fuck this shit."

"I know you're right, Adam, *but* . . ."

"She's dead. You two didn't even get along . . ."

"It's all my fault." I declared.

"*Bulllll*-shit!" He sang out in a loud, mean voice. "Don't you do this to yourself, man!"

I ignored him as I peered out the window and watched the night life crawl around. Because of the unusual heat, more people were hanging out.

We pulled into the parking lot. Adam shut off the engine and reached out for me before I exited the car. "Let it be."

I nodded silently.

I went up to see her.

She was naked on the slab in preparation for the autopsy. Her body was as white as snow as they drained the blood from her body. The coroner was dressed in his green garbs and rubber gloves, the surgeon's mask around his neck.

"I didn't know anyone else was coming to see her after her folks identified the body. I'm two days backlogged but I got orders to do her pronto." The coroner told me. "Understand she's a cop's wife. Too bad—she was a beauty."

I nodded. "Yeah, she was a beauty."

"Did you know her?"

"As best as a man can."

The coroner was taken back by my comment. "Hey, you're not . . ."

I looked him in the eye. "Not anymore."

Jesse opened the door of her Manhattan apartment. She stepped back startled. I stood in the doorway, bag in hand. She saw the condition of my face and reached out to touch it. "Mitch?"

I brushed by her and tossed my bag on the kitchen table. I went to the fridge and took out a beer. I opened it and pushed my head back to drink it.

"Mitch . . . what . . . what happened?" She circled me, afraid to come near me. I must've appeared like a completely different person to her. I was certainly acting like one. But I felt so much pain . . . so much anger.

I placed the cold bottle against my feverish forehead. She approached me cautiously. "Mitch?" I opened my arms to embrace her.

I kissed the top of her head. "Not so tightly . . . my ribs." I pushed her away gently.

"My poor Mitch." She said, tears streaming down her face. "What's going on?"

"I don't think I really know." I replied honestly.

"How did you get hurt?"

"Some guy I met." I touched my sore lip. "He has a helluva right."

"Are you in some kind of trouble?" She inquired bluntly.

I couldn't help myself—I laughed. "Ever since you left on Monday my life has never been the same. They torch my shop. Run me around in circles. Treat me like a punching bag. Yeah, Jesse, I think I'm in some kind of trouble."

"Why?"

"Because I was too happy. My life was too peaceful. Somebody had to remind me that there's still a real world out there." I ranted.

"I don't understand you, Mitch." She looked at me like I was a lunatic.

I shook my head. "Me neither."

She touched my hand. "Do you want me to take you to the hospital or something?"

I looked into her beautiful eyes and smiled. "All I need is some rest."

I put my arm around her and walked her into the bedroom. I plopped down on the bed. She helped me off with my sneakers and jeans. She saw my gun.

She stood up abruptly. Every muscle in her body constricted. "What's that?"

"What does it look like?" I took off the holster and put it in the drawer of the bedside table.

I tugged off my knit shirt and she cried out when she saw the bruises on my torso. "Oh, Mitch!"

"Get me an ice pack . . . please." I fell back onto the bed with a whimper.

She came back a few minutes later with a plastic bag filled with ice cubes. "Will this do?"

I took the bag and held it against my side. I grimaced from the pain.

"I think I should take you to the hospital."

"No." I responded.

"There could be some broken bones."

I shook my head. "I know the difference."

"What can I do for you?" She asked, evidently feeling helpless.

I glanced at her. "Nothing. I'm fine." I stretched out on the bed.

She put a pillow under my sweaty head. She held her hand against my forehead. "You're burning up."

"The air conditioner on?"

"Yes . . . it's not the heat, Mitch, you have a fever."

She went into the bathroom and returned with a bottle of Tylenol. She gave me two and I washed them down with the beer.

"Should I call Adam?" She asked, disturbed by her lack of experience in such matters.

"I'll go see him in the morning."

She sighed. "I'm worried about you, Mitch."

"Don't be." I tried to assure her.

"Who's doing this to you?"

"RayBeam." I replied.

"The videotape company?"

"Uh-huh." I yelped when I shifted my position on the bed.

"I don't get it."

"Video tape piracy. I stumbled onto it by accident."

"Why didn't you tell me?" She asked angrily.

"I really didn't figure it out until this morning."

"Well, let the police handle it." She said stubbornly.

"I am the—" I caught myself. "It's too late . . . it has become personal now."

"What're you talking about?" She was baffled by my statement.

"This is *my* problem."

"You're not a cop anymore, Mitch." She drilled into me.

"That's what I used to think, too."

"You're not making any sense." She snapped.

"Listen, these people . . . they think they can just fuck with anybody. Burn my store. Upset my whole life. They slap you down and think you'll just sit still for it. No way, Jesse. They started up with the wrong man. Now I have to finish it for them."

"Get off the macho number, Mitch. You're not that kind of man. That's why you split from the force. You didn't get off on breaking heads."

"The hell do you know how I was as a cop? You hardly knew me back then."

"Were you like *this*?" She sneered. "This was the way you acted when you tried to track down Kate's killer. You didn't think I noticed how preoccupied you were back then—did you? I felt like I was living with a stranger. You quit the force, yet you were still acting like a cop. It wasn't until I dragged you out of the city and to the Hamptons that you were yourself again."

I took in a deep breath and composed myself. "Don't Jesse . . . I'm not feeling very good. I'm sorry if I came on too strong. I'm hurting. I'm tired . . . cranky. Let's discuss this in the morning—okay?"

She sat down on the edge of the bed. "You're scaring me, Mitch. Are you sure there isn't more to it than you're telling me?" She rested her head on my stomach, peering up at me with her warm green eyes.

I ran my fingers through her blond hair. I felt like a prick. Sometimes I treated poor Jesse like shit. She was so good to me . . . too good. Maybe I thought I didn't deserve her affection. I don't know. I had left the force because I didn't know who I was anymore. I had played more characters than an actor. It had been hard to come home to my real life after spending time as a pimp or drug addict. Sleazeballs mostly—they were my specialty. It had been difficult going back to being myself—undercover cop Jeff Mitchum. I think I had lost him along the way. After I had won the lottery I just became a different character. A wealthy playboy with a house in the Hamptons and a beautiful model/actress squeeze. Only I wasn't really wealthy. It was just another facade. Maybe it was a blessing in disguise that all this was happening. It might bring me back down to earth to reclaim the real Jeff Mitchum.

I snapped out of my thoughts and saw that Jesse was still waiting for an answer. "I'm sorry, Jess. I feel like I'm trapped. They're coming at me from all directions. I don't have the whole picture yet so I don't know what to expect . . . I have to keep looking over my shoulder. You know what I mean?"

"You sound like you're scared."

I looked away from her. She was right. I was scared. But what was I afraid of? My adversaries? Or me?

The real Jeff Mitchum.

What if I didn't like him after I found him again?

12

FACE VALUE

FLASHBACK ... MORE BAD
memories. After Finkelstein had tipped me off about
the downtown dagger intruder, I immediately paid a
visit to the detective working on the case. His name
was Matrix. He had been recently promoted and was
still green around the ears. A handsome young man
with blond hair, blue eyes, and a squeaky clean
complexion; he didn't come off like he was from
Brooklyn as he had disclosed, but more like a mid-
westerner. I met him at a Greek coffee shop around
the corner from his precinct. He was dressed in a
black suit, gray shirt, and skinny tie. He had a
convertible hip hairdo that looked straight in the
daytime and punk in the nighttime. I detected a small
pinhole in his left earlobe—a pierced ear. Needless to
say, he didn't dare wear an earring while on duty.

After a short spell of sizing each other up, he
finally asked me what I wanted from him.

"Information." I replied.

"About the Dagger Intruder?" He asked. When I

phoned him to set up this meeting I had told him it dealt with his current case.

"That's right. We had a killing on the Upper East Side that seems to match his m.o.." I informed him.

He smirked. Then glanced out the window, his glass of iced coffee at his lips. "I checked up on you, Mitchum."

"Is that right?"

"The victim . . . she was your wife."

"*Ex*-wife." I accentuated.

He faced me, his icy blue eyes penetrating me. "I spoke with Finkelstein . . . told me you were going outlaw on this."

"Welllll . . . it is personal." I admitted.

"I don't blame you. I probably would handle it the same way. But I'm an extremist. I play at it real hard. Both on duty and off."

"I gathered."

"Really?" He seemed interested to hear what I thought of him. "Fill me in."

"You're a kid. You're ambitious but lack experience. You enjoy certain aspects of the job. Maybe the Jekyll and Hyde number turns you on. Establishment pig by day, punk rocker by night. At least the chicks get off on it. You wear an earring. You have a convertible hairdo that must've set you back some sixty smackers. Your favorite color is black . . . especially leather. You dig making it with handcuffs." I winked.

He laughed as he shook his head. "Not bad, Mitchum, but way off."

"Really?" I looked him straight in the eye.

He averted his gaze and pinched his earlobe. "You saw the hole."

I shrugged. "The chicks dig that shit."

He nodded. "I'm a musician by night." He confided.

"Ahhh."

He gulped down his drink, his eyes never leaving me. He put down the glass and wiped his mouth with a napkin. "To be straight with you, Mitchum, I was told to close you out."

"Finkelstein?"

He shrugged, not wanting to commit himself. "From somewhere."

"Come on, Matrix, we're both nonconformists."

"It's easy for you . . . you're cutting loose. Me. I'm just getting into it."

"Afraid?" I asked him, noting the trickle of perspiration on his forehead.

He gulped. "Nope."

"I could be a great help to you on this."

"This is a little different from your usual gig, isn't it?"

"Kid . . . I know the street." I asserted.

"So do I." He declared defensively.

I sat back in my chair with a grin. "Yeah . . . in your own way. But I've been there. Down among the scum. I know how they think . . . how they operate. Let me make you a star, Matrix. I'll help you nab him . . . it'll be your collar. I'm retired. I can go places you can't."

He pushed his head back and took me in. He was thinking very hard about my proposal.

"Don't worry, you won't get into any trouble. I'll protect you."

He scanned the coffee shop tensely. "I don't know, Mitchum."

I smiled. "But I do know. You need me, Matrix. I'll make it happen for you. The force only likes performers, kid. You deliver the goods and you'll make it. Otherwise. . . ." I squirmed up my face. "Otherwise you're shit."

He nodded. "What am I supposed to do?"

I smiled triumphantly. "Just leave it to me, kid, just leave it to me."

Jesse was already out of bed by the time I woke up. I sat up and a shock of pain streaked through me like a dose of electricity. I flinched and let out a moan.

"Mitch—is that you?" I heard Jesse's voice calling out from the kitchen.

She came into the room with a bright smile. She was wearing only panties and a skimpy tee shirt. She rushed to me and helped me sit up against the headboard. "You take it easy. I have breakfast going on the stove."

I kissed her. "Mornin', babe, you're too good to me."

She eyed my bruises and shivered. "You're a mess, Mitch. Does it hurt?"

"Only when I breathe."

"Did you sleep okay?"

I nodded.

"You twisted and turned a lot—bad dreams?" she asked as she sat on the edge of the bed.

"No."

"You should take it easy for awhile . . . stay in bed." She suggested.

I shook my head. "I have to go see Adam."

"That can wait."

"No, it can't." I retorted.

She didn't like my answer. "Starting already first thing in the morning?"

I grinned. "What's for breakfast?"

"Oh, shit!" She leaped from the bed and skirted into the kitchen.

She returned with a smoking frying pan and a smirking face. "Do you like your eggs well-done, Mitch?"

It was like going home again. The office looked like it had gotten a fresh paint job recently. Other than that, it was the same old place with the same old faces. All the guys gave me the look. That all-knowing smirk and wink. The Chameleon was back. The Man of a Thousand Faces. I had given Lon Chaney Sr. a run for his money. They all crowded around me. Patting me on the back. It made me feel good. I managed to slip into Adam's office after breaking up the small reunion. He was sitting behind the gray steel desk, his feet dangling off the edge. His hands were folded behind his head. No smile. Not even a hello. I nodded to him and shut the door.

Finally, he said: "Who did your face?"

"The pyromaniac."

"Did a good job."

"If you like what he did to my face, you should check out what he did to my ribs." I eased into the green chair next to his desk. "His name's Pike.

Adam picked up his phone and dialed. "Hey, Jack-off, run a name for me. Pike. P as in prick. I as in . . . oh, right, like the fish." He covered the mouthpiece. "Does this dude have a first name?"

"We didn't have that kind of relationship. He's definitely from Boston and did some time."

Adam repeated that info to Jack and hung up. "He's running it through now."

"Do you have anything for me?"

"On your friend Gage"

"He took Chloe with him to his Manhattan pad."

"Nice pad." Adam opened a file folder. "He just moved to a new place."

"Oh?"

"Yeah, bought himself a modest apartment in Trump Tower."

I whistled.

"The man knows how to live."

"What's the lowdown on him?"

"Full name—Brandon Gage. Forty-four years old. Married for eighteen years to Nicola, has a daughter, Chloe, aged fifteen. Has a home in East Hampton. That new pad in Trump Tower. Harvard Business School grad. Some family bread from his old man who was in real estate. Been the president of RayBeam for the past three years. He was in real estate for awhile. Then advertising. Turned a few companies around . . . including RayBeam. That wild man director, Sam Rayburn, almost ran it into the ground. He hired Gage to save it. Gage started acquiring cult films and porno. He's catching up with the big boys.'' Adam closed the file and threw it on the desk. ''Boy genius type with the Midas Touch.''

''Maybe he couldn't turn RayBeam around without getting down and dirty.''

''Piracy?''

I nodded. ''The man must have an enormous ego. He might've wanted to save face. Pull a DeLorean number.''

''Maybe.'' Adam stared up at the ceiling. ''But moving hot tapes . . . that can be tricky. The major studios are real uptight about that. Never mind the mob.''

''Montana still running that show?''

''Sure does.'' Adam lowered his gaze and looked me straight in the eye. ''Where do we go from here, Mitch?''

''I wanna talk to Montana.''

''You ain't a cop no more.''

''So?''

''So why would Montana wanna break bread with you?''

''Mutual interests. I don't think he would like someone moving into his territory.''

''Who says he don't know about it? Maybe the man made a deal with Gage. What then? He'll take you on one of his one-way trips, Mitch.''

I shrugged. ''That's a chance I gotta take.''

''Shit, you don't have to do a damn thing. Why are you doing this?''

''Somebody's out to get me, Adam. I don't like being beaten up. I don't like having my store torched. I don't like having my home trashed. And I especially don't like waking up next to dead bodies." I pounded my fist on his desk for emphasis.

The phone rang. Adam picked it up. "Yep—what took you so long?"

He started writing something down. "Good boy. Send it on up." He slammed down the phone and smiled at me. "Hunter Pike. Your good ol' boy. The man did three stints. One for playing with matches. Two for assault with a deadly weapon."

"Yeah, his fists."

"A torch for hire. Also does odd jobs. A former boxer. Never made it."

"A shooter?"

Adam shook his head and made a sour face. "I don't think so. He's just a tough guy. Breaks legs for Shylocks. Burns down ghettos. Real small-time stuff."

"He seemed to think I off'd the old girl."

"Really?"

"Un-huh."

"Well, murder does seem to be out of his league." Adam remarked.

"Unless Gage brought someone else in for that." I said.

"And didn't tip off Pike? I don't like the sound of that."

"Keep the jerk in the dark. The less info he has, the safer Gage will be."

"Maybe." Adam removed his feet from the desk and sat straight up in the chair. His face buried in his fat black fingers. "Everything fits except the murder. And where's the body?"

"Pike admitted to cleaning up the mess . . . my mess he called it."

"Do you believe him?"

"I think so." I expressed with reservations.

"It still doesn't gel . . . they had a perfect frame job on you . . . why clean it up?" Adam inquired.

I stood up and went to the dirty window. There was a traffic jam down on the street. Horns blasting. The noisy air conditioner couldn't drown it out. The entire scenario was as foggy as this window. "I don't know, Adam . . . I *just* don't know."

"Maybe I should make it official police business."

I swung around. "No . . . not yet. I can handle it."

"Mitch, you're not on the force—remember that. You don't carry a badge. You're a civilian. You have to abide by the rules."

"The same rules Gage is abiding by?"

He burned into me with his big black eyes. "You step on too many toes and I may have to drag you in. Gage is an important man in this town. He has a lot of honcho friends. Face it, the man's got big bucks and big bucks run the country."

Ignoring his warnings, I added, "I also need to talk with a former employee of Gage's. He might be my ticket to see him. His name's Victor Wesen . . . W-E-S-E-N. He used to sell for RayBeam. Disappeared after I complained about the *E.T.* tape mix-up."

"Where does he live?"

"Used to be in Queens somewhere."

Adam picked up the phone again. "Yo, Jack, me again. I need another one. Wesen . . . one 's'. First name: Victor like in victory. Check out motor vehicle. Need an address. Probably a Queens resident." He hung up.

I returned to the chair and sat down. "I need another favor. I want you to set up a meeting for me with Montana."

"No fucking way." Adam sliced the air with his hand.

"Either you do it or I go through the back door."

"And get your ass in a sling. That's playing it real smart . . ."

"Come on, Adam, do me a favor."

"I have been doing you a favor. A lot of favors, in fact." He complained.

"I have to speak with Montana."

"You go in without a shield, I don't know how you come out, Mitch." Adam cautioned me.

"I can handle myself." I declared.

He took in my bruised face and said, "You don't look like you're doing a very good job of it, man."

13

JESSE

JESSE SAT ACROSS from me at the small outside table. During the warm season, Manhattan's restaurants literally poured out onto the sidewalks. They set up tables outside for that Parisian touch. Nothing like eating an expensive lunch out in the open polluted air watching snail-like traffic and disgruntled New Yorkers sweep by. Always a pleasure. Jesse had a break in her cartoon dubbing schedule so I decided to take her out. Figured I owed her one for last night. She wasn't saying much. Just sipping her Diet Coke and lemon, her eyes closed, her face drawn to the sun's rays.

I was working on my second Amstel Light.

I was wondering how we ever got together. We were from two different worlds. I was from the other side of the tracks by way of blue-collar Brooklyn. She was from Westchester by way of Scarsdale and a lawyer dad.

I had first set eyes on her out in Amagansett. I was having lunch at the Lobster Roll restaurant with a young woman I had picked up at the nearby beach.

She was a coed with long dark hair and blue eyes and an incredible bod. Her name was Brenda. She was eating a lobster salad sandwich while I munched on a fried clam roll. We were halfway through lunch when Jesse entered the restaurant with a sandy-haired guy. My eyes were immediately drawn to her. She was wearing a long turquoise tee-shirt that covered her bathing suit. She had long blond hair and radiant green eyes. I recognized her right off the bat from her television commercials. They sat down at a table next to us.

We exchanged glances. She gave me a sly smile. Her companion turned around to see who she was looking at. I nodded. He acknowledged me and turned his attention to Jesse. He evidently asked her who I was. She shrugged and giggled, again flashing on me.

By this time, Brenda did a double-take herself. "A friend of yours?"

"Not yet." I replied, my eyes still stuck on Jesse.

Brenda waved her hands in front of me. "Hey, remember me?"

"I'm sorry." I snapped out of it.

"You're pretty intense, Jeff."

I took a swig of beer as I sneaked another glance at Jesse. She had just given her order to the waitress. She stood up, excused herself, and headed for the public phone.

I wiped my mouth. "Excuse me, I have to hit the head."

"Sure." Brenda said as she continued to eat.

I squeezed my way through the tables, Jesse's companion glaring at me as I passed. I encountered

her at the phone. She was waiting behind another
patron who was already using it.

I flashed a smile. "Haven't we met?"

She sized me up. "I don't think so."

"Are you sure?" I asked. "I've seen you before."

She laughed. "Maybe on television.™"

"Oh? Are you an actress?" I played dumb.

She nodded.

"I thought I knew you!" I exclaimed. "Commercials right? Those designer jeans. . . ."

She blushed in embarrassment. "Yes."

"Hi." I took her hand. "I'm Jeff Mitchum."

She shook my hand. "Hi, Jeff."

"My friends call me Mitch." I related.

"Okay . . . Mitch." She said. "My name's Jesse
Dillon."

"Jesse. I like it. Great name." I complimented
her. "Out here on vacation?"

"Just for the weekend."

I nodded. "I have a summer share myself."

"Oh, that's nice."

"Yeah . . . hey could we get together sometime?"

She giggled. "You sure don't beat around the
bush."

"Why bother? I find you attractive and I'm madly
in love with you." I kidded her. "I mean, I hope that
guy's not your old man or anything."

She was still in stitches. "You're something else!"

"So how about it?" I pursued her.

The phone was free.

"I have to make a call." She told me.

"Just a harmless drink sometime. Here or back in
the city."

"You live in town?"

"Sure."

She cocked her head to one side. "Are you somebody I should know?"

"Hell, no. I'm plain folk." I said. "I thought maybe you needed a break from your usual high-powered pals."

"Oh you did?" She was curious. "What do you do?"

"I'm a cop." I retorted.

"A cop?" She roared with laughter. "I would never have guessed it."

"I'll take that as a compliment."

"I really have to make that call." She turned to pick up the receiver.

I reached over and took the phone from her hand. "Hey, come on don't brush me off like that."

Her companion came up behind us. "Is there a problem, Jesse?"

I faced him. He was older than the both of us. Mid-forties. Handsome in that Ralph Lauren sort of way. Probably an actor himself. "She can take care of herself, pal."

"Mitch." Jesse pushed me aside. "It's okay, dear, I'll be right with you."

"Are you sure?" He asked, his eyes burning into me.

I smiled defiantly back at him.

"Go on back to the table." Jesse told him.

He reluctantly left us.

"The man's uptight. Should see his doctor about his Type-A Behavior." I said.

Jesse put her hand on her hip. "You know, you're very obnoxious."

I raised my hands. "I apologize. But I won't leave you alone until I get a commitment out of you."

She shook her head. "You're not my type."

I smiled. "You won't know until you've tried."

"Then you'll leave me alone?"

I placed my hand on my heart. "Scout's honor."

She took in a deep breath, her eyes all over me. "I admit, I'm curious."

"There you go."

She went into her pocketbook and pulled out her business card. "I don't usually do this. I mean . . . you're a complete stranger to me."

"At least you know you can't go wrong with a cop. You'll be in good hands." I winked.

"How can a cop afford the Hamptons?" She asked.

"When he wins the New York State Lottery." I replied.

"You're not serious."

"Dead serious."

"A lot?"

"Millions." I related.

"On second thought . . ." She grinned as she gave me her card. "I'll be in town next week."

"Thank you . . . I'll give you a call."

"Great. Now will you leave me alone?" She asked.

"Only temporarily." I smirked.

Later I found out she had also been very attracted to me. We met for that drink at an Upper East Side bar. It was the usual meat-rack crowd. After one drink, we left. I just had to get out of there. We took a walk down to the East River. It was an unusually cool summer's evening. We sat down on a park bench.

"I'm sorry about that place." I said.

"You seemed . . . so awkward . . . out of place." She observed.

I shrugged. "This dating stuff is pretty new to me. I recently split with my wife. Well, it's been a year now."

"Oh, that's too bad."

"It's not easy to be married to a cop. That's why I'm thinking of quitting."

"You really did win the lottery?" She asked.

"Yep. Didn't you see me in the papers? I made it on the cover of the Daily News. 'COP SHARES LOTTERY JACKPOT'."

"I didn't think anybody ever won." She announced.

"The odds are against you." I admitted. "But somebody has to win once in a while."

"What will you do if you quit the force?"

I shrugged. "I wouldn't mind moving out to the Hamptons. Get away from this stinking town."

"But you'll have to do something to pass the time."

"Yeah, you're right. All I know how to do is be a cop."

"How did you get into it?"

"My old man was a cop. And his old man . . . the same old story." I asserted. "I guess I'm not very original."

"What did your wife do?"

"A school teacher." I sighed. "A real boring couple. Not anything like your lifestyle."

"It's not as glamorous as it looks, believe me." She said.

"I guess work is work."

"You got that right." She laughed.

"What about you—ever been married?" I inquired.

She shook her head. "No . . . I've had some serious relationships, but . . ."

"Nothing clicked." I finished her sentence for her.

"I wasn't looking for any serious commitments . . . my career always came first." She stated.

"You're talking in the past tense. Have you changed your mind?"

"Yeah, I have. I wouldn't mind coming home to someone. It would be nice to share things with somebody, y'know?" She sounded lonesome. After a pause, she broke out laughing. "I'm sorry, I can't believe I'm saying these things . . . I mean, we *are* strangers."

I put my arm around her. "We may be strangers . . . but I feel like we've known each other for ages. Like we went through this already."

She chuckled, "You mean like in another lifetime or something?"

"I don't know much about that cosmic shit. Like I said, I'm plain folk."

That night we went back to her place and made love. I've been hooked ever since. She was a bit head-strong. Spoiled. Got whatever she wanted. Well, almost. She was still waiting for a marriage proposal.

I snapped out of it and came back down to earth. She opened her blue-green eyes. She was wearing a pink blouse and blue jeans. A little make-up. Her

long, slender legs folded under the table. She began
to pick at her salad. She wasn't much of an eater.

I took in my half-eaten hamburger and greasy
fries. It wasn't exactly as healthy as her lunch. "You're
very quiet today." I said.

She picked up a piece of lettuce and put it in her
mouth. Chewed it thoroughly. Swallowed. Took a
sip of her soft drink. "Just thinking."

"About what?"

"Nothing."

"Are you angry?"

"At what?"

"Me."

She eased into a smile and shook her head. Like
me, she was a thousand miles away. "You went to
see Adam this morning."

I wiped my mouth with a napkin. "Yeah."

"How did it go?" She inquired.

"Okay."

"You still keeping it to yourself?"

"No, of course not." I replied defensively.

"We used to be able to talk." She declared.

I shook my head. "Not really. You know that has
always been my little problem."

"I thought you were getting better. I haven't seen
you so tight-lipped since . . ."

"Kate's death?"

She cleared her throat and changed the subject. "Is
Adam going to help you?"

"Yep."

"I mean officially." She accentuated.

"Come on, Jes, let's talk about something else." I

said. "I was just thinking about the first time I met you."

The thought brought a smile to her face. "Yeah, it was love at first sight." She shifted gears again. "What's Adam going to do for you?"

I rolled my eyes. "You don't quit."

"What about the shop?"

"What about it?"

"Are you going to repair it?" She inquired.

"Of course."

"Shouldn't you be worried about that instead of sticking your nose into this video tape piracy nonsense?"

"I didn't start this thing, Jesse. They did."

She was annoyed at me. "What are you going to do for money, Mitch?"

"What're you talking about?"

"Don't act dumb with me. I know what's going on. I received a call from a credit service recently. It seems you're a little behind in your payments." She said unpleasantly.

"WHO CALLED YOU?!" I demanded to know.

"Mitch!" She snapped. "You know you've been living way over your head. Why didn't you come to me with your problems?"

"Because they're *my* problems." I retorted odiously.

"Your problems are our problems, Mitch." She stated. "I have money . . . I can help."

"No, Jesse." I cut her off. "I can take care of my own financial matters—thank you."

She shook her head. "Your foolish male pride." She dismissed me. "I think you're getting yourself all wrapped up in this to run away from your real problems.''

"This doesn't look like a real problem to you?" I waved at my bruised face. "I'm not running away from anything. Quite the opposite.''

"I don't think you should be doing your own police work on this . . . bring in the real police.''

"I'm as good, if not better, than your so-called real police.''

"Jesus, it doesn't take much to bruise your little ego.'' She asserted.

"Listen, I can't bring in the authorities now. I don't have enough evidence yet. I need to dig around a little bit. Something should shake loose.''

"Then you'll call the police in?''

I nodded. "I promise. I mean, I already have Adam involved. I'll be okay.''

"What does he think about you running around playing detective?''

"I think you two belong to the same fan club.'' I stated.

"No, we're just worried about you, Mitch.'' She said.

"Let's drop it . . . okay?'' I finished my beer and signaled the waitress for another one.

Jesse sighed dramatically. "Boys will be boys . . .''

I detested her when she came on with this attitude. "If you don't like it—you have a few options.''

She cocked her head to one side, eyes squinting. "You should learn to listen to people, Mitch. You always reject anything that doesn't jive with what you have in mind. That's real limiting. Tunnel-vision. You're smarter than that. At least, I hope so.''

The waitress came by with my beer. She was a dark-haired Hispanic. Attractive. Street-smart. She gave me a smile. I returned it. She scooted off. I followed her with my eyes. She seemed to have been poured into her black jeans. Soft, sexy flesh.

Jesse cleared her throat.

I felt embarrassed and took a swig of my beer.

"How is it, every time we have a little argument, your eyes begin to wander?" Jesse asked, unamused.

"Whaddaya talking about?"

"Your little waitress friend."

"What?" I shook my head and rolled my eyes. "Give me a break, Jesse. Talk about imaginations."

She leaned forward in her chair, eyes on my eyes. "Don't give me that, Jeffrey Mitchum. I made an investment in you. It's been over two years now, don't blow it on stupidity."

I waved my white napkin. "Truce."

She sat back and gave me her crooked grin.

I looked away and watched the steamy traffic along Second Avenue. After a while I turned back to her. "What do you want from me?"

"I just want to know the truth."

"What truth?"

"Do you want to stick it out with me?" She asked seriously.

"Yes."

"Then stop giving me a hard time." She said half-jokingly.

"You're the one giving me a hard time." I reminded her.

She laughed.

I joined her.

It was a no-win situation.

I recalled the time just after I had won the lottery and quit the force. My divorce had already gone through and Kate and I struck up a new friendship. Totally platonic. She had wanted us to remain friends. Jesse hadn't thought too much of the idea. We had been going for a few months and things were getting hot and serious. One night she had given me hell for having dinner with Kate. She had asked me to choose between her and Kate. What choice did I have? I went with Jesse.

Definitely a no-win situation.

14

LEGWORK

AFTER MY LUNCH with Jesse, I returned to her apartment where Adam had left a message on her answering machine. He gave me the Forest Hills address of Victor Wesen. He also arranged a meeting for me with Montana for tomorrow morning. Things were cooking. . . .

I vowed to take the subway to Forest Hills instead of my Porsche—the auto theft rate for the outer boroughs surrounding Manhattan island was quite high. Wesen's high-rise apartment was within walking distance of the subway station. Although quite humid, it was a pleasant stroll through this quaint neighborhood.

A doorman in a dark green uniform and cap stopped me from entering the building. He took his job very seriously. He wasn't very cordial, he just snapped: "What apartment, mack?"

I took the old geezer in. With his antiquated uniform, he resembled an over-the-hill bellboy. I flashed a smile and told him I was looking for Victor Wesen.

After sizing me up, he announced, "He ain't in."

"Really?" I pulled out my wallet and showed him a twenty. "I need to talk with him."

"You a friend?" He asked.

I thought it over for a second. "I think so."

"Friends don't have to bribe their way in, mack." The doorman stated.

"Come on, pops, I'm losing my patience." I said angrily.

"I told you—he ain't home."

"When will he be back then?"

He shrugged his beefy shoulders. "I ain't his keeper—y'know what I mean?"

"Listen, I'm not out to break his legs or anything. Even though I know some people who might be interested in doing just that." I conveyed.

"Is that a fact?" He could care less, this son-of-a-bitch.

I stuffed the twenty in his breast pocket. "Ring him. Tell him Jeff Mitchum is here to see him."

"I told you . . ."

I took hold of his lapels and pushed him up against the buzzer board. "I SAID RING HIM!"

The old-timer looked me in the eye and gulped loudly. "Hey, take it easy, sonny."

"*RING HIM!*" I commanded.

"You don't understand . . . ."

I reached down into my ankle holster and hauled out my Walther. I stuck the barrel against one of his nostrils and said, "I don't think you understand, pops."

"Sure . . . take it easy." He reached over and buzzed the apartment. "M-M-M-Mr. Wesen, t-t-there's someone here to see you."

"I'm not in!" I heard Wesen's voice reply.

I spoke up. "Vic, it's me, Jeff Mitchum. I just wanna talk."

There was a pause before he relented. "Come on up."

I released my grip on the old man and put my gun away. The poor bastard was shaking like a leaf. He backed away from me, his hands raised. "I-I-I'm sorry, mister, Wesen told me to keep all visitors at bay."

I gave him another twenty. "Buy yourself a drink, pops."

"S-S-Sure . . . gee, thanks."

I took the elevator to the twelfth floor. I walked up the apartment door and knocked. A few moments later the door opened a cracked. I saw Wesen's brown eyeball staring out at me. "Mitch."

He unlocked the door and stood before me dressed in a burgundy terry cloth jump suit.

"Hello, Vic, it's not easy to get in to see you. Your doorman just shit in his pants."

"Sorry about that, come on in."

He locked the door behind me as I sauntered into the immaculate apartment with its white carpeting and fine furnishings. The television set was on in the living room. A porno tape was playing. Marilyn Chambers was choking on John C. Holmes' monster dick.

Wesen picked up the remote control and shut it off. *Insatiable* was wiped from the screen. In its place, a "Leave it to Beaver" rerun.

"Can I get you anything?"

"Black Jack on the rocks."

He went into the spacious kitchen and returned a few minutes later with two glasses of Jack Daniel's. He handed me one. I took a sip and said, "Great place."

"Your shoes." He said.

"Huh?"

"House rules—they have to come off."

I looked down at my black Reeboks.

"The white carpeting . . . my wife." He explained.

"Sorry." I sat down on the plastic-covered sofa and removed my sneakers. I noticed he had on a pair of fluffy slippers.

He sat down on the edge of the adjacent love seat. He appeared extremely uneasy. He hugged his drink like it was the Holy Grail.

"Long time no see, Vic." I announced.

"I was canned." He admitted. "Wasn't making my quota."

"Is that a fact?" I took another sip of my drink. "Your friends torched my shop, Vic."

He was about to take a drink when he froze in mid-motion. He glanced up at me through the top of the glass. "I don't know anything about that."

"I didn't say you did."

"I told you . . . I was let go."

"Right after I got that *E.T.* tape by mistake . . . was that the reason?" I inquired.

He took a long pull of his drink. "So you figured it out?"

"Maybe."

"That's what I was afraid of."

"Afraid of what?"

"My boss . . . it went all the way to the top. That's why I split."

"I thought you said you were fired?"

He stood up and went to the window that opened onto a terrace. "I would've been . . ."

"So you walked away and been hanging low ever since." I stated.

He faced me. His hands were shaking. "I wake up every morning wondering if this will be my last day . . ."

"Why don't you get out of town if you're that afraid?" I asked him.

"How in hell can I explain that to my wife?" He hissed. "She doesn't know anything. I just told her that they let me go."

"Whaddaya doing for bread these days, Vic?" I wondered.

"Savings . . . my wife has a good job. I'll get back into selling soon. But not video fucking tapes." He declared as he finished his drink.

"So Gage is definitely behind this whole operation—correct?" I asked him point-blank.

"He'll have me killed. . . ." He put down his glass and went out on the terrace.

I followed after him. He gripped the railing as he looked out over the view. With his back to me, he said, "I'm scared, Mitch. Scared shitless."

"So you think they're capable of murder?" I tested the waters.

He craned his head around to eye me. "What the fuck do you think?"

I shrugged. "I don't know, that's why I'm asking."

He turned his body around and rested his back

against the guard-railing. ''I think that man is capable of anything.'' He uttered bitterly.

''How do I get to see him?'' I inquired.

''Stay away from it, Mitch.'' He warned me.

''They torched my shop. One of his gorillas worked me over. I can't stay away from it, Vic.'' I informed him.

He shook his head. ''How in hell did we get into this mess?''

''How deep were you into it?''

''Here and there. I mean, I knew what was going on. That tape you got by mistake . . . that was my fuck up. That's why I . . .'' He cleared his throat. ''Retired.''

''So you didn't tell them about me getting the tape?''

''Nope. I don't know how they found out.'' He said.

''I do.'' I retorted. ''From me.''

He closed his eyes. ''Don't tell me . . .''

''Yeah, I wrote them a complaint. Jesus, was I stupid. It just didn't dawn on me about piracy. It was the farthest thing from my mind. I thought it was a legit mistake.''

He brought his hand up to his face. ''I don't believe you did that.''

''I guess I fucked up. I only hope I didn't put you in jeopardy.'' I said.

He peeked at me through his fingers. ''We'll soon find out—won't we?''

It was a new modern office building on Madison Avenue and Fifty-fifth Street. Montana Enterprises, Inc. had office space on the thirty-third floor. It was another wet morning, a light mist in the humid stagnant air. If my shop had been open it would have been packed to capacity.

The pretty receptionist greeted me as soon as I got off the elevator. She was sitting behind a sweeping bleached wood desk. The company's big M logo on the wall behind her. She was dressed elegantly in a white linen outfit. She was all teeth and blue eyes.

"Good morning, sir, may I help you?" She asked mechanically.

"Yes, I have an appointment with Mr. Montana. My name's Mitchum."

She glanced down at her date book and checked off my name. "Oh yes, Mr. Mitchum, please be seated."

I wandered over to the brown leather sofa and sat down. There were some company propaganda handouts on the smoked glass-top table. I picked up the slick pamphlet and began to leaf through it. It featured Montana's various holdings. He seemed to be into many diverse trades. A cement company. Commercial sanitation. And the most interesting one of all, VidHots, a pornographic video distribution company.

"Mr. Montana will see you now." The receptionist's voice disturbed me. I looked up and she was standing before me. "Just this way."

I trailed after her down the carpeted corridor. We swept by several buzzing offices until we got to the end of the hallway. She opened the door and I entered the room. It was quite impressive. Very high-tech. Not at all what I expected. Montana was standing behind his huge, spotless desk. He was of medium height and weight, dressed meticulously in an Armani gray silk suit. His hair was dark brown and combed straight back. His eyes were brown and warm, his gleaming smile appeared super white against his suntanned face. I shook his hand and sat down on the leather chair before the desk. I must've looked like a bum in my safari jacket and jeans.

"How about a cup of coffee?" Montana offered.

"No, thank you."

He waved his hand at the receptionist and she left the room.

"Now, Mr. Mitchum, you wanted to see me about some urgent matter." He pushed himself back in his chair, his manicured fingers crossed across his flat stomach.

"Well, I had hoped we could speak . . . candidly."

He narrowed his thick eyebrows as he gazed intensely at me. He probably wondered if he could trust me. Finally after a few long seconds of silence, he asked: "You're an ex-cop?"

"Yes."

"You're no longer associated with the force?"

"No, sir." I replied politely.

"You're not wired?"

I shook my head.

"I must warn you, Mr. Mitchum, my office is monitored. Anything said here can be used against you if the need arises."

I cleared my throat. "I understand that."

He smiled. "A police detective . . . Adam Hayes . . . made the appointment with me."

"Yes, I asked him to."

He put the palms of his hands together and brought

them up to his lips. He still seemed puzzled by my visit. He sat there like a mild mannered priest waiting to hear my confession. I could feel the muscles in my stomach tighten as nervous perspiration beaded on my forehead. The silence was killing me.

"Go on." He said.

"It's about . . . videotape piracy."

He shifted in his chair, the expression on his face unchanged.

I continued, "I stumbled onto something. I should tell you—I run a video rental store out on the Island."

"Yes, I know."

"You know?"

"Of course." He declared.

I swallowed with some difficulty, my throat dry.

"A glass of water?" He asked.

I scanned the room. "Okay."

He stood up and went to the wet bar in the corner of the room. He poured water from a black pitcher into a glass, added ice, and brought it to me. I thanked him and drank some down.

He leaned against his desk before me, hands on his hips. He waved me on.

"Well, I had ordered a movie from RayBeam. A porn tape. A customer bought it from me and later returned it because it wasn't a porn tape at all. It was a copy of *E.T.*"

He nodded, seemingly more intrigued by my tale.

"So, I wrote them a complaint letter and put the tape aside. A few weeks later I get a note from them explaining they had fouled up in duplication." I shrugged my shoulders. "Then I just forgot about it. A few months pass and somebody torches my shop and some gorilla works me over. He wants the tape back. So I figured I had accidentally become involved in some kind of video piracy scam.''

"Why are you telling me this?"

"Come on, Montana, nobody moves hot tapes without you knowing about it."

He stood up and went to the floor to ceiling window behind his desk. He stayed there for awhile, a blinding halo around his body. He turned to face me. I couldn't make out his features in the harsh glare from the window. "Are the police involved?"

"Unofficially."

"Have you done some investigating on your own?"

"Yes."

"What have you come up with?" He queried.

"Brandon Gage is involved." I announced.

Montana returned to his desk, sat down on his swivel chair and rolled over to a computer terminal. He punched in some data. The machine wheezed and sounded whistles for a few minutes then printed out something. Montana tore off the hard copy, scanned it, and handed it to me across the desk. It was a data sheet on Brandon Gage. In the corner was a thermal-printed photograph of him.

"I already have this information . . ." I said after reading it. "And you're missing some updated facts. He's currently residing in Trump Tower." I returned the data sheet to him.

He smirked. "He's above suspicion."

"Nobody's above suspicion, Mr. Montana."

"Spoken like a true cop." He said.

"Ex-cop." I accentuated.

He swung around in his chair, his back to me. "You've brought me some valuable information."

"You weren't aware of this, then?"

"I'm afraid not." He admitted candidly.

"I'm surprised."

He turned around to face me. He wasn't smiling anymore. "We have a common interest in this little . . . problem."

"I would think so."

"I would like to get to the bottom of this. I could help you. I have many resources at my disposal."

I shook my head. "I don't want you to call out the troops, Montana. I'm in pretty deep with this. I want to go against Gage."

"You won't get very far legally, Mitchum."

I stood up. "Who said anything about legalities? I told you, I'm not a cop anymore. Nobody's backing me up on this."

"You have me." He proclaimed.

"I came here just to see if this was your operation. Not to have you get involved."

"I believe I have the manpower to infiltrate Gage's operation. Gage knows who you are. In fact, you're a target. It's silly of you to assume you can go against him." He said, obviously amused by my quest.

"No, Montana. This is mine. If I fail . . ." I finished off my water and slammed the glass down on his desk. "If I fail, it's in your court."

He smiled. "If you need anything—you call."

I nodded.

"I can act more swiftly than your cop friends. I also want to be kept posted on this, Mitchum. I don't think this can be a major operation. I would've known about it if it were. There have been other instances when I had to lean on these amateurs to keep them out of the business. I can do that just as easily with RayBeam.'' He snapped his fingers. ''And they'll cut loose.''

''I have a feeling there's more to it than just that.''

''Oh?''

''Like murder.''

''That's what business is all about.'' Montana got up and stuck his hand out. I took it. ''Your hands stopped shaking, Mitchum.''

I smirked. ''I guess I was a little nervous about how this meeting would turn out.''

''If you ever want a job . . .''

I raised my hand. ''No thank you.''

''Most of my employees are ex-cops, you know.''

''And working cops, too.'' I winked.

He laughed. ''I like you, Mitchum.''

''That makes my day.'' I exhaled dramatically. ''You don't know how much that makes my day, Mr. Montana.''

15

RED RAIN

I STOOD in the gold and pink marble lobby of Trump Tower. There was much traffic as tourists and shoppers swooped onto the multi-level arcade of boutiques and fashionable shops. It was kind of like an indoor Rodeo Drive. Still dressed in my safari jacket and jeans, I wandered through the premises among the designer outfits and tailored suits. I checked out the sales office. Real estate agents sat behind desks within the glass facade trying to unload the multimillion dollar suites. I checked my watch. Three o'clock. I had been standing around here since I left Montana's office this morning. I felt relieved that he was not involved with RayBeam. Otherwise there was a good chance I wouldn't have legs to stand on anymore.

I was hoping to catch Chloe. I decided not to go to the front desk and ask to see her. I didn't want her father to know that I was in town. Not yet anyway. I was still trying to figure out my approach. Do I just walk right up to Gage in his office and confront him? No, that wouldn't work. It may throw him off-guard though. But what if he has Pike hanging around? He would let him loose on me and that would be the end of that. No, I had to think this through thoroughly.

Then I saw her.

Chloe.

She was heading out the front door. Next to her was a tall man. Gage. He was dressed in a knit shirt and khaki trousers. His arm around her shoulders. They were having a conversation. She was wearing a black outfit of mini-skirt and tee-shirt and high-laced sneakers. She looked like rock singer Madonna. I followed after them.

The rain had stopped, the sky still gray but bright. They set off up Fifth Avenue. I walked slowly behind them. Trying to keep my distance. They crossed the street onto Fifty-seventh Street going west. They were still engaged in chit-chat. She stopped at one point and skirted over to the window of a shop. She waved her father over and both entered the store.

I went over to the Charivari storefront. The window display had a cluster of male and female mannequins dressed in Japanese-styled white outfits. Very avant-garde. Very New Wave. Very Chloe.

I smiled. She will have a field day in this store. I entered the shop and eyed the salespeople behind the register desk. One strange looking young man dressed in a bath sheet, and a sexy lean blonde with cropped hair and even sharper features stood passively beneath several monitors showing a Godzilla movie.

The girl checked me out, fluttered her foot-long eyelashes, and went back to her daydreaming.

I went deeper into the store. It was a modern design in the minimalist style. Electronic pop music was being piped through the speakers. Another sales-person asked if I needed any assistance. I just stood there dumb-struck as I tried to figure out the sex of the person. I just shook my head and smiled.

I found Chloe with her dad at the clearance rack. She seemed excited by some of her clothing finds. At one point she stood before Gage holding a garment and telling him the price when she spotted me. Before she could react I held a finger to my lips, turned on the balls of my feet, and shot out of there.

I ran across the street to wait.

About twenty minutes later they came out of the shop with a bag and headed back to Fifth Avenue. I tagged along, still across the street from them. I saw Chloe turn her head around to see if I was behind them.

I wanted to make sure she knew I was here. I had to get to her. Alone.

They went to the entrance way of Trump Tower. There, Chloe gave her dad the bag and kissed him. He entered the lobby while she walked north on Fifth Avenue.

I remained on the street adjacent to her. I wanted to make sure Gage wouldn't come after her. She checked out the F.A.O. Schwarz windows and then crossed the street and hurried towards Central Park. I was about a block behind her as I watched her ma-neuver expertly through the traffic of taxis and horse-drawn carriages.

She made it to the park and strolled up one of the many tree-shrouded paths. I ran after her.

She must've heard my footsteps because she swung around and greeted me with open arms. I embraced her and felt her warm peck on my cheek. "Hiya, Mitch, whaddaya doing here?"

"Came to see if you're okay."

"Sure I'm okay." She stared up at me with squinty eyes. "What happened to your face?"

"Cut myself shaving." I took her arm and we started to walk on. "Was that your dad?"

"Yeah."

"Good looking guy." I said.

"He's okay." She wasn't going to give an inch.

"You left kind of unexpectedly the other day."

"Yeah, my dad found out that my mom split. He didn't think I should be left alone or some such bullshit." She related.

"Have you heard from your mother?" I inquired.

She shook her head.

"Isn't that weird—not hearing from her?" I pursued the matter.

"I guess." She didn't seem too bent out of shape about it.

"What did your father say about it?" I wondered.

"Not much. Just that she would be gone for a while."

"Where did she go?" I asked.

"He said she went to Europe."

We stopped by a bench and sat down. There was an elderly lady sitting across from us. She gave us a dirty look and left, muttering under her breath.

"So she went to Europe." I said.

"Yep."

"Strange isn't it?"

She shrugged her shoulders. "I'm glad you came to see me."

I rubbed her crew cut and smiled. "Wish I had a watermelon, wish I had a watermelon . . . " I chanted.

She pushed my hand away and laughed.

"Chuck, we gotta talk."

She laid her azure orbs on me. It only made it more difficult.

"I want to tell you what's been going on. With me. Me and your father."

"My father?"

"Yeah. You see, he's involved with something that affects me."

She appeared puzzled. "Whaddaya talking about?"

"Somebody burned my shop. An arsonist. He's the one who worked on my face." I pointed out.

"Why?"

"I'm getting to that. You see, your father hired this arsonist."

"WHAT?" She gazed at me like I was out of my mind.

"Just be quiet for a second and hear me out. He hired this guy, a hoodlum, to obtain a video tape that I got by accident. The guy figured that if he torched my shop he would destroy it. Only I didn't have it in the shop. I had it at home. So he came after me to get it. Worked me over. He didn't get it. I still have it. But he's still out to get it and me."

"I don't understand." She was having trouble following me.

"It's your father. He's involved with video tape piracy. It's illegal. And he wants to make sure I don't spoil things for him."

She shook her head. "No, my father wouldn't do that." She declared.

"And your mother." I cleared my throat. "She isn't in Europe."

She shot up and glared at me through teary eyes. "Why are you saying these things?"

"Chloe—please listen to me. I'm telling you the truth."

She was shaking her head violently.

"Chloe . . . your mother . . . your mother is dead."

She covered her ears with her hands sobbing loudly. "NO!"

"I'm sorry, Chloe, but it's true."

"NO—YOU'RE A LIAR!!!" She screamed and ran off.

"CHLOE!" I hurried after her.

I caught up with her and grabbed her arm. "Chuck—don't."

She pushed me away. "I NEVER WANT TO SEE YOU AGAIN!"

A small gathering of spectators crowded around us. One black dude cried out, "Leave the little girl alone."

"Mind your own business!" I shouted back at him.

Chloe backed away from me. She appeared frightened of me. So filled with hatred. I reached out to her. "Please, Chuck, let me help."

She turned and rushed away.

A couple of kids blocked me. "Lay off her, motherfucker!"

I tried to push them out of the way, but more bodies surrounded me. I lost sight of her. I snapped out of it and found myself in a middle of a rat pack. They were a mean-looking bunch of Hispanic thugs.

They were dressed in ragged denim jeans and vests decorated with silver studs. They wore spiked leather wrist bands and other motorcycle paraphernalia. A few of them had baseball bats.

I raised my arms. "Hey guys—what gives?"

They started to giggle. The ringleader started tapping my chest with a bat. "Whaddaya doin' with the little piece of pussy, man?"

"I don't want any trouble."

"Maybe we want some trouble, white bread." He pushed the bat towards my stomach but I grabbed hold of it and whipped it out of his hands. I swung the bat around me, making the gang members back off.

One of them came up to me with a bat. He held it out in front of himself, hopping from foot-to-foot. "Let's get it on, man!"

He came out swinging and I counter-blocked with my bat. The gang formed a circle around us as we battled. It must've looked like something out of an old gladiator movie. Our bats cracked loudly. After a few clashes, I found an opening and drove his head all the way home. He dropped his bat and just stood there shaking his swirling head. His left ear was bright red. A few moments later he collapsed like a rag-doll to the ground.

The gang watched in dismay.

I broke the circle and ran deeper into the park to find Chloe. I still held the bat as I craned my head around to make sure that nobody was following me. I felt safe and ditched the bat.

I brushed by a few people as I ran on.

Then I spotted her.

She was sitting alone on a bench. I went over and sat down next to her. She was staring straight ahead.

"Chuck?" I touched her hand.

That was when she fell over into my lap, the handle of an ice pick sticking out of her ear. I felt my heart skip a beat as I held her head in my lap. I looked up when I heard a scream. It was a black woman. She covered her mouth with her hands, her eyes bulging from the sockets.

I looked down at Chloe, her body still warm in my arms, and felt the pressure building up, stronger and stronger, inside me. Until I thought I would explode.

I glanced up again and saw a small crowd swelling up around us. And Pike was among them. His eyes on me as he backed away . . . disappearing into the pack. Sirens sounded in the distance.

But I couldn't leave her. I just sat there. And waited. Even later when the downpour came. And the people continued to watch, their umbrellas drawn. I waited.

Chloe had been so alone in life, I thought she would have liked me there after death.

16

THE HAUNTING

THEY HELD ME in the interrogation room. Adam stood off to the side. Homicide Detective Romanus was across the table from me. He was standing, his foot up on the chair. We'd been going at it for over four hours now. Romanus' brown eyes eating away at me. I couldn't stand staring at his pockmarked face any longer. I just wanted to get the hell out of there. I resented them treating me like a common criminal.

"Okay, let's run through it one more time." Romanus sighed.

Adam and I exchanged glances. Then I took in Romanus. I never liked the man. The hard-nosed type. He was a cop through and through. Everybody was suspect in his world. He had come out of Internal Affairs. That was where he belonged. He seemed to get off on grilling his fellow cops. We had a few run-ins in my time. Our last outing had been an especially painful one. I had been already off the force so he couldn't touch me. But it appeared like he was going to make up for our last encounter this time around.

145

"Why don't you give me a break, Romanus." I balanced my chair on its hind legs. "You know I didn't do it."

"I have a dozen witnesses that say they saw you arguing with the girl . . . that you were chasing her . . . grabbing her." Romanus stamped out his cigarette angrily.

"We weren't arguing. I had just laid on some bad news to the kid. She was upset. She didn't want to believe me. I wanted to console her." I explained.

"She was in tears . . . shouting at you . . . telling you to leave her alone."

"I told you . . . she was upset." I repeated.

Romanus swung the chair around and sat down backwards on it. "Now lemme get this straight. You told the kid that her mother was dead—that right?"

"Uh-huh."

"Yet, the woman's own husband told us that she's away in Europe."

"He's lying . . . I have it all on video tape."

"That tape again . . .." Romanus rolled his eyes.

"I've seen it—Mitch is telling the truth." Adam injected, his back against the wall, arms folded.

Romanus nodded. "Where is this tape?"

"I have it."

"I'm curious to see it."

"Well, if you ever let me out of here I'll get it for you." I told him.

"The witnesses said you were . . . angry . . . abusive . . . even violent." He persisted.

"Bullshit!" I hissed.

"I got a kid in the hospital with a concussion. His seven buddies tell me you assaulted him with a bat."

He continued to pour on the facts. He was enjoying every squirming minute of this.

"That was in self-defense, Romanus." I tried to remain cool.

"They claim they were only protecting the girl." He claimed.

"Yeah, right. Just a bunch of nice kids taking a leisurely walk through the park with baseball bats." I quipped.

"They said they had just been throwing a ball around . . . had themselves a little game."

"Right." I retorted. "Never mind they probably got records going back to infancy."

"They all have prior juvenile offenses." Adam informed us.

I smiled broadly at Romanus.

He didn't seem amused. He stood up and wandered over by Adam. He wouldn't look at him. He asked, "Whaddaya doin' here, Hayes, this ain't your case?"

"I'm on my coffee break." Adam answered.

Romanus eyed him intensely. "One phone call and you're out of this room."

Adam didn't even bat an eyelash.

I got up and stretched. I looked down at myself repugnantly. My jeans were covered with blood stains. "Come on, Romanus, I'm beat."

He swung around and pointed at me. "I don't think you realize what kind of trouble you're in, Mitchum. Just because you used to be a cop don't mean you're above suspicion. Hardly. Not with your abominable background. I recall our last meeting . . . a very unpleasant affair. I never liked you, cowboy. It's your kind that gives this department a bad rap. The best thing that ever happened to us was when you quit the team.''

I marched right up to him, standing face to face. ''You should really do something about filling in those craters, Romanus.''

He shoved me away. Adam grabbed hold of him. ''Chill out, Romanus.''

I returned to my chair, the smile never leaving my face.

Romanus lit up another Carlton and went back to his corner. He sat down and studied me for a few minutes. Then he said, ''I have enough evidence to arrest you for murder. Do you understand that, Mitchum? Have you already forgotten the law? Or maybe you were never enough of a cop to know the law in the first place.''

''Kiss me.'' I shook my head and eyed Adam. ''Do you believe this asshole?''

''I have dozens of witnesses that say you and the girl had an argument and that you were with her at the time of her death.''

''After the time of her death.'' Adam specified. ''You have no witness that said he saw Mitch perform the act. Nor are there any fingerprints on the weapon. Now don't you find that a little bit strange, Romanus? If Mitch killed the girl why would he bother to wipe his prints if he stayed put until the police came around? Huh?''

Romanus kept his eyes on me as Adam spoke. A cigarette dangled from his thin lips. His right eye half-closed from smoke irritation.

''Yeah.'' I said. ''Why would I even stick around

if I killed her? What do I look like—a schmuck? Not everybody thinks like you, Romanus.''

"Hayes—get your friend outta here before I tear him apart."

I blew him a kiss. "Love you, too, sweetheart."

Romanus abruptly reached across the table to grab me. I shot up. Adam came between us. "COOL IT!"

"Just remember one thing, Mitchum. You're still my prime suspect. And believe me, I'm going to nail your ass to the wall if it's the last thing I ever do."

"It might just be the last thing you do, Romanus." I sneered.

Adam pulled at me. "Let's go, Mitch."

"I'm going to try to convince that kid to press charges against you." He added.

I turned around and our eyes interlocked. Romanus was steaming. He meant business. He still hadn't figured out his limitations. Some day I'll fill him in.

Adam and I walked out of the building to the parking garage.

"Dumb . . . real dumb, Mitch."

"He's an asshole."

"Maybe. But the man has power. The people at the top, they like Romanus. He made a lot of friends while he was in Internal Affairs."

"Not among the real cops."

"I'm talking politics here, Mitch. The man is being groomed—you know what I mean?"

"Just what we need . . . another jerk-off commissioner."

"He's tough and he's stubborn. He gets what he goes after. Now he wants your ass."

"I'm shaking." I got into Adam's car.

After he got behind the wheel he said, "I would be if I were in your shoes."

I looked him in the eye. He was serious. "Thanks for the warning."

"You better hand over those tapes."

"First thing."

He started the car.

I yawned loudly.

"Get some rest. You're going to need all the energy you can muster up. I just got word from a buddy in Queens. Your friend, Wesen, took a head-dive off his terrace last night."

"WHAT?!"

"I didn't want to mention it back there for obvious reasons. Romanus would have a field day with you over that one."

I was stunned. "Poor bastard." I muttered. Then I struck the dashboard with my fist. "That was my fault!"

"Chill out, Mitch." Adam tried to settle me down. "The department says it was suicide. Wesen's old lady contends he was depressed for months since he lost his job."

"I don't buy it. He was helped . . ."

"Maybe . . . maybe not."

"Everywhere I go, bodies follow . . ."

"It keeps gettin' closer and closer . . . I'm worried about you, buddy. Maybe I should take you into protective custody." Adam suggested.

I hit him with a hard glance. "Are you fuckin' crazy, man?"

"It's for your own good. You better start worrying

about your own tail, friend. There's some deep shit going down and you're in the line of fire.''

We took off. We didn't say anything for a few blocks until I said, ''Adam.''

''Yeah?''

''I didn't mention something back there.''

''What?''

''I saw Pike in the park. He was there in the crowd.'' I informed him.

''Are you sure?'' He inquired.

''Yep.''

''Why didn't you tell Romanus?''

''Why bother? He's not looking to find the real killer in this case. He's just looking to burn me.'' I replied.

''He's still smarting from the last time you locked horns.'' Adam reminded me. ''He really wanted to bring you down—remember?''

I gazed out the window. I didn't want to remember. It still left a sour taste in my mouth. But I had no choice. All I could think about was my inquiry into Kate's murder. . . .

After my agreement with Matrix, I had started to delve deeper into the Dagger Intruder case. I had been knocking on doors, asking questions. One of the victims had agreed to see me. She was a young Hispanic woman with a small child. Unmarried, she rented an apartment on East Thirteenth Street.

We sat at her kitchen table with a cup of coffee and I began my examination.

She was about twenty with long black hair and nice features. She was self-conscious about her bad complexion and would hide her face behind her hands as she spoke. She was wearing a skimpy halter top, her shapely breasts poking through. She crossed her legs and squirmed in her cut-offs throughout our meeting, a steady stream of cigarette smoke swirling around us. Her name was Rose Vasquez.

"This intruder," I began, "you said he was black?"

"That's right. A big dude. Very skinny but tall . . . like a basketball player."

"What did he do?"

She dragged on her cigarette and let the smoke out real slow. "He climbed through the window in my son's room." She stopped, obviously upset by her memory. "Thank God Stephen didn't wake up. I don't know what that scumbag, eh—" She caught herself. "I'm sorry."

"It's okay." I smiled. "Go on. Being a cop I've heard a lot worse."

"Well, he came through Stephen's window."

"That's where the fire-escape is—correct?" I interrupted her.

She nodded, her face fuzzy from the cigarette smoke. "Yeah, the super should've put a gate on the fuckin' thing. He has since. Natch. But anyway, this nigger comes into my house and starts going through my dresser drawers . . . my pocketbook . . . everything."

"Did you hear him?"

"Yeah. At first I thought it was a rat raiding my trash can in the kitchen." She stopped for a breath. "I have rats in this stink-hole. So I put the pillow over my head to, y'know, block out the racket. But then it keeps moving."

"Moving?" I asked.

"From room to room. The rats . . . they don't usually do that. They just want to eat and run—y'know what I mean? So then I get like, y'know, real scared. I sat up and cried out. 'Who is that?' I said."

"And then what?" I inquired.

Then the tears began. "I'm sorry."

I took her hand. "I understand."

"It's just . . . so real." She sobbed.

Her little boy came running out to see what was the matter with his mommy.

"Go back to your room, Stephen!" She ordered.

The kid hesitated, evidently concerned about his mother.

"It's okay." She told him. He disappeared promptly.

She blew her nose. And after a few minutes composed herself enough to continue her story. "He ran into my room. He had this . . . this knife."

"A dagger?"

She shrugged. "It was long and sharp."

"Maybe an ice pick?" I inquired.

"Huh?"

"An ice pick. Did it look like an ice pick?"

She thought it over. "Yeah, sort of, I guess. He waved it around to scare me. I wasn't wearing much . . . just my underwear. He jerked me out of bed and put the blade to my neck."

"Did he say anything to you?"

"Yeah . . . 'Shut up!' He called me names. Bitch. Cunt. Stuff like that."

"Then what did he do?"

"He . . . s-s-smacked me hard across the face. I tasted blood. I started to cry . . . beg for my life."

"Did you resist at all?"

"I guess. It wasn't much use . . . he was too big."

"Then what?" I urged her on.

"He did it." She said flatly.

"Did it?" I inquired.

She looked at me with her bloodshot eyes. "He raped me."

"How?"

She eyed me with disgust. "HOW?!"

"I mean, what were your positions? On the floor . . . on the bed? From the front? Did you see his face during the act?"

She covered her face with her hands. "From behind . . . on the floor. I never really saw his face."

"Where was the weapon at this point?"

"I felt it at the back of my neck." She answered.

"Here?" I put my hand at the back of my neck.

She removed her hands to see. "No—more like here." She reached out and touched the side of my throat with her long fingernail.

"He didn't cut you at all?"

She shook her head.

"Then what happened?"

"He took some more things and left."

"What were you doing?"

"Crying." She replied.

I took hold of her hand. "I want to thank you for telling me this. I really appreciate it." I said sincerely.

"Has this help you any?" She asked.

I smiled. "Yes, it has." I stood up and took out my wallet. I gave her a hundred dollar bill.

She looked at the crisp new bill then up at me with

sorrowful eyes. "You don't have to do that."

"Yes I do . . . please take it. Buy yourself something nice. You deserve it."

She grabbed hold of my hand and kissed it, uttering something in Spanish.

I never forgot that poor young woman. Just another victim. But she had broken my heart. I knew when I caught up with the bastard I was not only going to think of poor Kate but also this woman and her child. Meeting up with the creep was what had made Romanus blow his cork. Some nonsense about taking the law into my own hands. . . .

"You think Pike did it?" Adam's voice disturbed my musings and I snapped out of it.

I shrugged. "Maybe we should dig deeper into his background. Find out if he likes to dress up. Maybe he's a transvestite." I snickered. "Just what we need, another Norman Bates."

"His records don't show anything like that. And one other thing bothers me, Mitch. Gage. Why would he off his wife and kid?"

"Maybe Pike has gone outlaw . . . Gage lost control of him."

Adam shook his head. "Doesn't click with me."

"Me neither." I admitted.

"Well where do we go from here?" Adam was stumped.

"Gage. He's the only one with the answers. And I'm dying to hear his excuse for why his wife isn't showing up for Chloe's funeral."

"Maybe we should give Romanus the straight dope."

"No fuckin' way." I snarled.

"You really enjoy giving him a hard time, don't you?"

"I owe him one from the last time. That poor kid, Matrix." I said bitterly.

"He knew what he was doing." Adam remarked.

"Yeah . . . he believed in me. I let the poor bastard down." I asserted remorsefully.

"You can't cry over spilled milk, Mitch. That was then, this is now."

I faced Adam. "Then how come my latest troubles keep reminding me of back then?"

"Ghosts." Adam said. "Just ghosts."

BRUTE FORCE

ADAM DROPPED ME OFF in front of Jesse's high-rise apartment building. It was just after eleven o'clock and the night shift doorman was on duty. He eyed me suspiciously.

"Evenin', Mr. Mitchum."

"Juan."

"Saw you on the news tonight."

"The news?"

"Yeah, you made the first page of the *Post*, too." He held up the rag to show me. There was a picture of Chloe and me on the park bench. The headline screamed: **FIFTEEN-YEAR-OLD GIRL MUR-DERED IN PARK**.

I took the paper from him and scanned it. They ran an old departmental photo of me on the inside. I shook my head. "Jesus, they've already found me guilty."

"Yeah, I just couldn't believe what they said." He remarked honestly.

I gave him back the paper. "Have a good one, Juan." I headed for the elevator.

"You too, Mr. Mitchum." He said after me.

I got off on the twenty-first floor and fumbled with my keys as I stood before Jesse's door.

Suddenly, the door creaked open.

"Jesse?"

She was against the door. The apartment dimly lit.

I leaned over to peck her when I noticed the bruise on her cheek. "What in hell happened?"

She had been crying. Her eyes were red and there were black streaks down her face where the mascara had run. She wrapped her arms around me and hugged me tightly.

"Who did this?" I demanded to know.

I closed the door and made her sit on a kitchen chair. I crouched down and held her by the shoulders. "Jesse, sweetheart, are you okay?"

She nodded, her eyes filling up again. "He wanted the tape."

"What?"

"A man. An ugly man. He pushed me around. Slapped me. Kept asking for a tape." She sobbed.

"What did he look like?"

She shook her head. "Ugly."

I stood up and said, "Pike."

She glanced up at me with her tear-filled eyes. "Who is he?"

"He's the one who worked me over. I'm going to kill that son-of-a-bitch. I can't believe he would do such a thing to you . . . goddamn animal." I uttered through clenched teeth.

"What's this tape he wanted?" She inquired.

"That pirated tape I told you about. The one that can help prove my case against Gage."

"Well, he went through all our video tapes. He was like a maniac. He didn't find what he came for. That's when he punched me." She held her face.

I looked at her bruise more closely. "Any loose teeth?"

"No."

"I better take you to the hospital for a check-up."

"I'm okay, Mitch." She said bravely.

"I don't know about that, Jes. How about if I call your doctor—whatshisname?"

"I'm okay, really."

"You don't look okay." I remarked.

"Mitch." She blew her nose. "Where did you hide the tape anyway?"

"In my car."

"Oh, Mitch, you better go check it."

"I'm not going to leave you like this." I cracked open some ice from the freezer and wrapped it in a towel. I placed it against her face. "Just hold it there."

"I saw you on the news . . . the murder . . . what's going on?"

"It's all tied in with Gage and the tape. At least with that tape I'd have some proof of my allegations. Without it . . ." I didn't even want to think about it. I needed both tapes to save my ass. So far, I hadn't filled Jesse in on the homemade tape of Nicola's murder for obvious reasons. I didn't want to hurt her anymore than I already had.

"Mitch, you better go make sure he didn't get the tape if it's that important. I'll be fine. Go. Just hurry back."

I hesitated but knew she was right. "Okay, babe."

I went into the bedroom. The drawers were spilled out on the floor. I found my gun in the rubble. I put it in my pocket and went back to the kitchen. "Now I'm going to lock this door. Don't open it for anybody. Understand?"

She nodded.

I kissed her and left the apartment, securing both locks behind me.

I took the elevator to the basement floor—the entrance to the parking garage. I found the young black attendant sitting in a small booth reading a glossy porno magazine. When he looked up he seemed startled to see me. "Eh, Mr. Mitchum . . ."

"My car. Take me to it." I commanded.

"Why . . . sure." He gulped. "Just this way."

I followed him up the ramp to the next level. We walked for quite a bit before we came upon it. I opened the door, leaned over, and groped under the seat.

They were gone!

I checked again and again. I stood up and eyed the attendant. "Who was here?"

"You missin' sometin, Mr. Mitchum?" He asked with the whites of his eyes glowing in the dark.

I came up to him. "WHO WAS HERE?"

"I don't know whatcha mean." He backed away.

I grabbed him by the collar of his blue shirt and rammed him against a car. "I'LL TEAR YOUR HEAD OFF IF YOU DON'T TELL ME THE TRUTH, KID!"

"What's wrong with you, man?!" He stared at me with his fluid eyes.

I roughed him up again. "How much did he palm you?"

"I don't know what the fuck you're talkin' about!" He persisted.

I pulled out my gun and held the snubbed weapon against his nose. "You wanna start breathing through three nostrils, kid?"

"YOU'RE CRAZY!" The attendant shouted.

"HOW MUCH?" I repeated my question.

He squirmed beneath my hold. "I didn't know what he was goin' to do . . . "

"HOW MUCH CAN YOU BE BOUGHT FOR?!" I wouldn't let up.

"He slipped me a Grant." He retorted with a heavy sigh that made him sound like he was deflating.

"FIFTY BUCKS!" I released my grip and backed off. I put the gun away. I took in a few deep breaths. My heart pounding in my chest. I realized what I was doing. I was taking out my frustrations on this poor kid.

"You won't tell nobody, will yah, Mr. Mitchum? I'm sorry. Here." He held the fifty in his hand.

I didn't dare look at him. "Get the fuck outta here!" I shouted with disgust.

"I'm sorry." He didn't get the message.

"GET OUT OF MY FACE!" I barked.

He ran off.

I locked the car.

I went back upstairs and found Jesse where I had left her. She sat there with the ice pack against her face.

"He got what he wanted." I said and plopped down on the chair next to her. I cradled my face in my hands, elbows on the table. I didn't have anything without those tapes. I was so foolish. I should've handed them over to Adam long ago.

Jesse touched my arm. I brought my hands down and looked at her. I had a lot of explaining to do to her. I didn't even know where to start.

"I'm sorry about your friend." She said.

"Chuck?" I shook my head. "Poor kid. She never had a chance."

"The news said that you were arrested."

"No, I'm a suspect but I wasn't arrested . . . not yet, anyway." I related.

"Oh, Mitch, what's going on?" She asked with pleading eyes.

I took her hand. "Somebody's really doing a number on me."

"Why you?"

"Why me? I've been asking myself that ever since I got dragged into this mess. Why me? Was it fate that I got the video tape by mistake? Who knows, Jesse. Now I don't even know if I'll ever get the answers." I responded bitterly.

She squeezed my hand to reassure me.

"I'm so sorry you had to get involved." I told her.

She gave me another smile.

"Don't worry, I'll get out of this somehow." I said, not believing a word of it.

She put the towel aside. The swelling seemed to have gone down. There was still a brownish-blue bruise. I reached over to touch it. Her skin was cold. Her sore eyes watched me sadly. I took her face into my hands and kissed her gently on her mouth. Her skin tasted salty from the dried tears. We got up and walked together into the bedroom. We stretched out on the bed, our limbs entangled.

I started from her head and worked my way down,

covering her with kisses. We exchanged no words. We were like two wounded creatures holed up in our little lair. Cut off from the cold, abrasive world.

We undressed and made love. It was a long and heated session. It seemed more than a matter of days since we had been together like that. Before the nightmare had struck. Before I had ever set eyes on Pike. Before I had come to know Chuck. It had been that wild and wonderfully drunken night. That time before my world turned upside down.

I drained my mind until it was free of thoughts. I wanted to concentrate on our lovemaking.

I remained inside her after I came. It was like we were one. And that made me feel good . . . for a while anyway.

But then the memories came back . . . flooding my head. Ghosts, Adam had called them. How right he had been. . . .

Matrix met me one evening at a downtown rock club. I was the oldest dude in the joint. A loud and nasty punk group was spitting on stage. We met at the bar along with assorted youngsters in their leather jackets and spiked hairdos. Matrix was dressed in his own black-on-black get-up of 501's and a tight spandex shirt with a chest full of glistening silver zippers. His hair was standing on end, a skull earring hanging from his ear. He was wearing heavy, black work boots, his arm wrapped around a skinny, shaggy-haired lady.

"I talked with the Vasquez woman!" I shouted into his ear while he nursed his beer.

He faced me. "Didn't you already read the statement she gave me?"

"Sure." I replied. "But I wanted to hear it for myself."

"Did you get anything out of her that I didn't?" He asked.

I shook my head. The band had stopped playing but my ears were still ringing. I wore a pair of jeans and a white tee-shirt, my hair in disarray. I stood out like a sore thumb.

Then a woman came out on stage dressed in a floral housecoat. She wore fifties-styled eyeglasses with flaring frames. The audience started to boo her noisily. She started her comic routine.

"Where do we go from here?" Matrix inquired.

"It's him. He's the one. I can feel it in my bones." I declared.

"But can we nab him?"

"Don't worry about that. If he's out there, I'll track him down."

Matrix craned his head around to face the stage as the audience voiced their disapproval. There was the performer pouring chocolate syrup down her naked ass. People began throwing things at her. "She's too much." He said.

I shook my head.

Matrix leaned over and stuck his tongue down his girlfriend's throat.

I yanked on his shirt. "I'm getting out of here."

He acknowledged me.

I hurried through the club and managed to make good my escape. There was a horde of leather vampires waiting to get in. I pushed my way through them and made it to the street.

Matrix came out after me. He said, "Pretty cool, huh?"

"That's not exactly the word I would use." I retorted. "Where's your girlfriend?"

He shrugged. "She's not my girlfriend."

"Do you always shove your tongue down strange girl's throats?" I inquired.

"Only if they ask for it." He replied seriously.

We started walking down the murky street. He had a beer bottle in his fist.

"Well, I will admit it's a place that nobody will ever see us together in." I stated.

"One thing I wanted to ask you, Mitch. I mean, here I am supplying you with confidential records. What if they catch on?" He asked with concern.

"Don't even think about it." I dismissed him.

"But what *if*? It could mean my job . . . . my whole future."

I halted and sized him up. "You backing off?"

"No . . . not exactly." He said unconvincingly.

"I warned you up-front, Matrix, once you commit yourself—that's it. There's no walking away from it." I told him.

"Why not? Who set the rules?" He asked defiantly.

I gave him a cold eye. "I made the rules, boy."

He backed down. "I don't like where this is going."

"Where is it going?"

"Whaddaya goin' to do when you find him?" He asked.

"What do you think?" I threw it back at him.

"That's what scares me." He admitted frankly.

"You sure dress tough, why don't you start acting tough." I said.

He took a pull from the bottle, the beer's foam running down his stubbled chin. "I don't like this."

"I knew it." I shook my head. "I just knew it!" I knocked the bottle from his hand and it fell to the ground with a loud crash. "YOU'RE A CANDY ASS!"

He stood there gapingly, his hands limply at his sides. He pushed back his head, his eyes clouding up. "FUCK YOU!" He snarled.

I walked away from him before I did something I would regret.

He caught up with me a few blocks later. "I'm sorry, man." He sobbed. "I'm scared . . . at least I can admit it!"

I stopped in my tracks.

I felt his hand on my shoulder and swung me around. Tears were streaming down his baby face. I embraced him and he wailed in my arms like a young boy.

I accompanied him home that night. He lived in a shabby tenement building in the East Village. A studio apartment that smelled like a sewer. The walls were covered with rock posters, a top-shelf stereo system was in the corner. Two three-foot speakers were on each side of his mattress that was spewed on the splintered wooden floor.

I confronted his roommate there.

"Are you out cattin' around again?" He asked Matrix. Then he took me in. "A little older than usual . . . what are you a chickenhawk?"

"Shut your face!" Matrix told his roommate.

His friend eased up. About the same age as Matrix, he had untidy dark hair and was wearing only his Jockey shorts.

Matrix faced me and said softly, "Thanks, Mitch, I'll be okay now."

"You sure?" I asked him.

He nodded. "Don't worry, you can count on me."

COUNT ON ME . . . COUNT ON ME . . . His voice echoed inside my head. I shot up and found myself in bed next to Jesse. I was soaking wet. Luckily, I didn't disturb her sleep.

I got out of bed and went into the living room. I poured myself a full glass of Jack Daniel's. I plopped down onto the sofa and took a stiff drink.

I toasted to Matrix and all the other spirit invaders. Jesus, was I carrying around a lot of heavy baggage.

I realized what was happening to me now was connected to my investigation into Kate's death. Somebody sure didn't want me to forget. But who was it? Romanus . . . murder . . . the ice pick and me caught in the middle of everything—the same ingredients from the last time. But I had caught up with the killer back then. . . .

Hadn't I?

18

DEEPER THROAT

WHEN I WOKE UP, I found myself on the living room sofa. My empty glass was on the floor at my feet. I stood up with great difficulty, my back and limbs stiff. My head ached, my brain swelling painfully against my skull. It must've been all the excess baggage inside me bursting to get out. All the spirits swirling around my head.

I shuffled into the bedroom where Jesse was still asleep. I stood over her. Her face was puffy, the bruises more pronounced. She wouldn't be modeling for awhile. Luckily she was only dubbing that cartoon these days.

I went into the kitchen and started the coffee maker going. I went to the front door and retrieved the *New York Times* from the doormat. I scanned through it until I came upon my photo on the first page of the second section. Next to it was a high school photo of Chuck appearing very straight-laced. She looked so young . . . so innocent. I slammed the paper down in disgust. When I glanced up Jesse stood before me.

I could barely look at her.

"My face . . ." She said sadly. "It's worse."

"He did a nice job."

"I'll have to call the agency and tell them to cancel some assignments." She said monotonously.

"I'm sorry, Jess." I tried to change the subject. "How about if I make you a nice big breakfast?" I asked gleefully.

She brushed by me and opened the freezer. She took out a cold mask and placed over her face. "I'm not very hungry."

I grabbed her arm as she whisked by me. "Jess."

"I'm going back to bed. Turn on the answering machine—I don't want to be disturbed." And with that said, she returned to the bedroom.

"Great, just great!" I hissed.

I poured myself a cup of coffee and sat down at the table. With my face all over the local newspapers and television news, I was going to have a tough time continuing with my investigation. It also hindered any chance for me to get close to Gage. I was going to need help. The department was out of the question. Poor Adam would have enough to do just to keep that goddamn Romanus off my back. No, I'd have to look elsewhere for assistance. . . .

Montana.

I eyed the clock. It was just after ten in the morning. I went to the phone and dialed his number. A sexy woman's voice answered.

"Montana Enterprises."

"Mr. Montana please." I said. "Tell him, it's Jeff Mitchum."

*　　*　　*

The Mercedes stretch limo was waiting for me in front of Jesse's apartment building. The dark-suited chauffeur opened the door and I joined Montana in the plush back seat. He was dressed in a white linen suit, blue silk shirt and tie. He greeted me with his dazzling smile as the car took off.

"I appreciate this, Mr. Montana." I said as I opened the collar button of my shirt and loosened my tie. I made sure I dressed up this time so I wouldn't look like a vagabond next to the dapper crime boss.

"No problem." He said in his laid-back manner.

"I guess you've heard the news."

"Yes." He smiled. "You're a celebrity."

"Hardly the attention I wanted right now." I sighed.

"A messy business." Montana said distastefully.

"Now I'll never be able to get to Gage." I shook my head in despair. "This media blitz will surely send him into hiding."

"Perhaps." Montana responded serenely.

"Gage managed to get those tapes I had." I related.

Montana started working on his manicured fingernails. "I've done some investigating of my own."

"Oh?"

"You're right about Gage. He's got a number of illegal tape transfers running around. High quality stuff. Seems to have inside sources at the major studios. I still don't know how he did it without me finding out about it." Montana complained. "Admittedly, a few outfits go unnoticed. But not an operation on such a major scale."

"I wonder why he's doing it. I mean, he's supposed to be legit."

Montana laughed. "You're pretty naive for an ex-cop, Mitchum."

"I don't know about that."

"Don't take offense. I was referring to your ignorance of the American corporate mentality."

"Does it all come down to the almighty dollar?"

Montana took me in with his brown eyes. "Money isn't everything. But power is."

"Power and money—aren't they the same thing? You can't have one without the other."

"There are plenty of people with money who have no power." Montana explained.

"And vice versa." I added.

"Now you're beginning to understand."

"So Gage needs money for power. I thought he already had plenty of both."

Montana gazed out the window and said, "You never have enough."

"You're right—I am naive." I admitted.

He sized me up and asked, "You'd just settle for money, wouldn't you?"

I shrugged. "I just want to be comfortable."

"Power doesn't interest you?"

"Never did."

"Now I'm beginning to understand you."

"And I you." I replied, our eyes interlocked.

Montana smiled and averted his eyes. "Now, how can I help you?"

"I want to get to Gage." I retorted.

Montana nodded. "Like you've said—it will be difficult now. But there is a way. A backdoor of sorts."

"That's me—the backdoor man."

We pulled up in front of a Forty-Second Street porno cinema. The chauffeur got out of the car and opened my door.

I looked to Montana for an explanation. He had a shit-eating grin on his face.

I got out and stood dumbstruck at the curb.

The chauffeur shut the door and went around to the driver's seat.

The rear side window rolled down. I saw Montana in the corner staring out at me.

"I don't get it." I said.

"You wanted to get to Gage." Montana said. "This is the backdoor I was telling you about."

"What?"

"Zoe Savage." He said, then the car swept away.

"Zoe Savage?" I repeated to myself. I turned around and glanced up at the movie marquee. It read:

Zoe Savage
in
X-TRATERRESTRIAL
After meeting this earth woman,
the last thing he wanted to do
was go home!

19

SPERM COUNT

THE MOVIE WAS SHORT and painless. An *E.T.* rip-off with sex, the extra-terrestrial in this picture was a well-endowed blond stud who befriends a nymphomaniac played by Zoe Savage. She goes on to teach him some of earth's kinkier practices. It followed the plot of the original pretty closely. I wondered if Spielberg had caught it. If he had, a lawsuit would be inevitable. It was pretty funny in spots and the sexual action was quite graphic. It had the usual porn wind-up when the semen hit the fan.

Zoe Savage had picked up the reins of Marilyn Chambers as porno's hottest new All-American Girl. She came off rougher around the edges, with her gravel voice and buxom figure. She also seemed more street smart and shrewd. You knew this chick had been around the block a few times regardless of her peaches and cream complexion.

As I watched the spectacle, I wondered why Montana led me here. Zoe Savage. How would she lead me to Gage? Just because he distributed some of her movies on tape didn't mean anything to me.

After the flick, I ventured out into the hot steamy sunshine. The street was buzzing with all kinds of sleazy characters and well-dressed businessmen. I took a few steps and turned around to look at the theater. I read the marquee over and over again.

And then it finally sunk in.

Was Gage having a fling with Zoe Savage? Even the thought of it blew my mind! The great American businessman meets the All-American porno star. Why not? I had never read anything about it in the gossip columns. Gage must have kept it tightly under wraps. I would think it would be embarrassing for him if it ever came out. Might tarnish his super-clean reputation. But to knock off his family for a woman? That was hard to swallow. That was when divorce came in handy. It saved a lot of people from going to the electric chair.

I hailed a cab and went to see Adam. I found him slumped over his desk looking like he had aged ten years since I saw him last. He glanced up at me over the frames of his reading glasses. He yanked them off and sat back in his chair, his folded hands behind his head. As usual not a peep out of him.

I sat down on the edge of the desk. ''Pike got the tapes, Adam.''

He still didn't utter a word but I could read his reaction in his eyes. Bad news.

''And I found a way to Gage.'' I informed him.

No response.

''Zoe Savage.''

Finally, ''Who?''

"The porn actress."

"What does she have to do with Gage?" He asked, his eyes hitting me with a big fat question mark.

"They . . . you know . . . got a thing going."

"You mean like an affair?" He arched his eyebrows.

"Precisely."

"Yeah, right." Adam shook his head, not believing a word of it.

"I got it from a reliable source." I smirked.

"Who might that be?"

"Montana." I replied.

That changed his mind. "You're shittin' me?"

"Nope." A smile glaring from my puss.

"Zoe Savage . . ." He mused.

"Makes it more interesting, doesn't it?"

Adam struggled to his feet and went to the window. He stood there. I could almost hear the gears turning inside his head. From behind I saw just how much he was out of shape. The layers of fat hung at his sides, his twig legs bent at the knees from supporting his ballooning torso. I hated to see such self-destruction. Adam had always been slim-hipped and barrel-chested. Now he was a physical wreck standing there passively like a grazing cow.

He turned to face me, hands on his hips. Yellow fluid veiny eyes. Sad eyes. Tired eyes. Unblinking and emotionless. "How would she be able to help us?"

"Gage has kept this thing under wraps. I now have an in."

"Exposure?" Adam asked.

I nodded. "He certainly would be interested in talking it over with me—yes?"

"But does it mean anything now that his wife and kid are outta the picture?" Adam continued to toss the problem around.

I shrugged. "Supplies a motive for the murders."

"He offs his wife and kid for this broad?" He shook his head vigorously. "No fuckin' way."

"It's something."

"It's nuthin!" He appeared angry at me. At my stupidity. He collapsed in his chair. Almost glaring at me. "Romanus has been workin' somethin' fierce to prove you're guilty. He has enough for a warrant. But not enough to bring you to trial. The D.A.'s office is on his back to deliver. He doesn't have much to go on . . . except for you. That tape might've saved your ass but now . . ."

"I'm up shit's creek without a paddle." I finished his sentence for him.

"Somethin' like that."

"Do me a favor." I asked of him.

He jerked his chin at me. "Whaddaya want?"

"Give me as much as you can find on Zoe Savage. Where she lives. Any shady dealings. The whole score."

"Montana might be more helpful to you in that respect. The mob and porn are one and the same." Adam stated wisely.

I thought it over, then said, "I don't want to strain my relationship with him."

Adam chuckled. "I'll bet."

"I have the feeling he knows the outcome already and is just leading me on." I confessed.

"You think he's involved?" Adam inquired.

I threw up my hands. "I have to trust him."

"You trust nobody, man." He asserted.

"I trust you." I maintained.

He nodded. "I'm still a cop and you're venturing into dangerous grounds. I can't tag along much longer. Otherwise Romanus will staple my ass to yours and string us both up."

"Why does he have such a vendetta against me? Doesn't he forget anything, for chrissakes?" I shot up and began to pace the floor.

"He'll never let up on you for that last number. He wanted you so bad then. That's why I'm concerned . . . he's just gonna keep on comin'."

"But I'm such a nice guy." I jested.

Adam threw his head back to laugh. "Yeah, right. You only make it worse with your cocky, wise-guy lip."

"Romanus can go fuck himself. Did you hear that?" I asked loudly in case Romanus had the office bugged. I wouldn't put it past him.

Adam roared.

I sat down again and there was a few minutes of silence. We just stared at one another, knowing we had so little in my defense. Finally, I said, "Pike ransacked the apartment and worked Jesse over."

Adam perked up. "She okay?"

"She'll live. But this Pike guy won't as soon as I catch up with him." I threatened.

"Don't even joke about it."

"I'm not joking!" I snapped. "The man's dead."

Adam looked me straight in the eye and declared, "Then I'll personally collar you for murder, tough guy."

I stood up with a heavy sigh. "Chill out, Adam.

Just get me the info on Savage.'' I went to the door and froze. I craned my head around and asked, ''When's the funeral?''

''Monday mornin' '' Adam related. ''Cemetery's out on the Island.''

I said, ''I don't know if Chuck would've liked that.'' And left.

The more I thought about Romanus, the more I thought about those scenes from two years ago. My investigation into the Dagger Intruder case had been going nowhere. It seemed he had stopped his act for a while or perhaps had taken it on the road. Whatever the case, nothing had been happening. It was a frosty, bone-chilling day when I met Matrix in Washington Square Park. I sat on a bench, my arms wrapped around myself. I wore a leather bomber jacket and cords, my booted feet freezing. Matrix showed up a half-an-hour late. He was decked out in his usual black suit and a long tweed overcoat that inched down towards his heels.

''You're late.'' I said.

He shrugged, vapor streaming from his mouth. ''What can I tell you—I'm working.''

''And I'm not?'' I asked nastily.

''Give me a break, Mitch, stop tearing into me. So we're at a standstill—what can I say? These things happen. You should know that better than I do.''
He sat down next to me and cupped his hands as he blew his hot breath into them. ''Too fucking cold.''

I scanned the deserted park. It was too cold for everybody it seemed. ''Listen kid, I'm sorry. You're right, I should know better than to blame you.''

"He'll begin again . . ." He said, then caught himself. "I'm beginning to sound like a fucking vampire. Here I am waiting for a vicious rapist, probable murderer, to strike again!"

I nodded. "It's sick . . . you can't help yourself . . . everybody gets caught up in it. The good guys . . . the bad guys . . . what's the difference?" I stood up and gazed down at the kid. "I was getting so close . . . I could smell him."

Matrix looked at me blankly. He still wasn't cop enough to understand me. He had a long way to go. "The pressure's on for me to deliver, Mitch."

"Don't worry about that. You just keep your eyes and ears opened. We'll nab this sucker."

"What if he isn't the man you've been looking for?" Matrix inquired.

I didn't answer him. "Call me when you have something." I walked off.

"Mitch!" He shouted after me.

I stopped in my tracks.

"What if he isn't your wife's killer?" He persisted.

Again, no answer. I walked on, my face numb from the cold. I had already asked myself that very same question countless times. What if . . . ?

When I reached the outskirts of the park I encountered Jesse. She stood there in her mink coat, her long hair blowing across her red face.

"Jess?"

"I followed you here." She told me.

"Why?"

She shrugged. "Just out of curiosity."

I approached her, but she backed away.

"What's going on, Mitch?"

I smiled innocently. "Whaddaya talking about?" I tried to make light of the matter.

She laughed insincerely . . . like the trained actress she was. "I thought it might've been another woman. And I was right in a way."

"What?"

"It's her . . . Kate . . . you won't let her go." She said, her eyes glassy from the cold.

I sighed. "Listen, it's too cold to talk about it here."

"When will it stop?" She inquired. "When do you stop playing cop? She's dead, Mitch. Period. There's nothing you can do to bring her back. You were divorced for chrissakes! I don't understand you."

I looked away from her and watched Matrix slink away.

"Who's that? A contact . . . a cop?" She asked.

I faced her. "He's handling a case down here. I'm helping him out."

"A case involving Kate?"

"Why are you doing this?" I asked.

"I'm losing you, Mitch. You're drifting away. I talk to you and you're not there. Do you know how frustrating that is? Let the police do their job. You should concern yourself about getting your own life in order."

"I have plenty of time for that." I retorted.

"And what about me?" She cocked her head to one side and waited for my reply.

"You know I love you, Jesse. Sure, I'm preoccupied right now. But I have to do this . . . for her . . . for me." I stated.

"Well, I can't take any more of this. . . ." She turned and walked off.

I caught up with her. "Jesse—please." I took hold of her arm and swung her around. She had tears flowing down her cheeks.

"I'll leave it up to you—choose between her or me." She snapped angrily.

"She's dead, Jess. There's no choice." I conveyed.

She shook her head. "Don't you see? She's still alive inside you. You're keeping her alive by this . . . this investigation of yours." She embraced me. "Let her go, Mitch, let her go."

I held her in my arms tightly. I knew she was right.

But I was so close . . .

20

THE SEND-OFF

THE WEEKEND PASSED

peacefully and without event. Jesse and I had spent most of the time together. She was feeling better. We didn't talk about my current dilemma. We acted like we didn't have a worry in the world. The only reminder was Jesse's bruises. But the swelling was down and most of the unsightly damage was hidden behind sunglasses.

It had been a while since we were in town together, so we made up for lost time by hitting some museums and shops. I bought myself a tropical-weight navy blazer and khaki trousers to trade off on my washed-out jeans and safari jacket. The beach bum look was fine for a resort town but not the city. Besides I needed something appropriate to wear to Chloe's burial. Although, Day-Glo shirt and pants would've been more to her liking. I couldn't get over how much of an impression she had left on me. We had known each other for only a matter of days. Maybe we had something in common . . . or we possessed the right chemistry. I guess I would never really know.

"A penny for your thoughts." Jesse offered while she caught me wandering off. We were sharing an ice cream sundae at an outdoor cafe on Fifth Avenue.

I smiled. "Nothing."

Now she smiled. "It's never *nothing* with you."

"You're right." I took her hand. She looked great today in her cotton sundress. I adored her freckled shoulders, and the sexy slope of her bare neck. "You look delicious."

"Yeah, right." She adjusted her sunglasses. "It must be the shades."

"The swelling is gone." I related. "You look like my old Jesse again."

She giggled. "Are you trying to seduce me, Mr. Jeff Mitchum?"

When we got home, I swept her in my arms and carried her into the bedroom. We laughed all the way to the bed. I slipped the dress over her head. She was naked beneath except for a pair of skimpy panties.

I removed my clothes and joined her in the bed. I kissed the bruises on her face tenderly . . . then worked downward. I took her nipple into my mouth and sucked gently. I felt her hands groping me . . . down my back . . . cupping my buttocks.

She pushed me onto my back and climbed on top of me, her legs straddling me. She leaned over and ran her tongue across my hairy chest. Before long she shifted position, her behind in my face, as she worked on my throbbing member. I felt the warmth of her mouth on my genitals. Her musk swirled around me as I tongued her.

Then the pressure built up in my loins and I let go as I climaxed vehemently.

Afterwards, we lay in an embrace. She nibbled my earlobe as my fingers probed her. Her back arched when she came, her teeth sinking into my flesh.

I held my ear. "*Ouch*!" I yelped. A small trickle of blood oozed from my wound.

"I'm sorry . . . " She sighed with contentment.

"Getting rough in your old age." I quipped.

"You know how carried away I get . . ." She said with a sly smile.

I got out of bed.

She rolled onto her side. "Where're you going?"

"I have to call Adam."

She made a sour face.

"I have to go to the funeral." I said.

She lay flat on her back, her knees up, her sex beckoning me for some more lovemaking. "If you'd rather talk to Adam . . ."

I took her in and said, "I'll call him later."

Adam and I stood away from the small crowd that circled the grave site. There were a few news teams hanging outside the gate of the private Farmingdale cemetery. Cameras on top of trucks, zooming in for a close-up of the fine wood casket.

Adam passed on those thermal prints I had made of the video tape to Romanus. I had given them to Adam for the lab to check out last week. But they were much too grainy to work with. They had blown them up, only making them worse with the numerous scan lines. Maybe it would pacify Romanus for awhile. Or maybe it was already too late. I had a feeling Romanus had already made up his mind about me.

I kept my eye on Gage. He was a tall, handsome man. Gray temples. Trim. Well dressed in a black pinstripe double-breasted suit. He stood by an elderly woman. Probably his mother. No sign of Nicola. Natch. He had told the reporters that she was too grief-stricken to attend the ceremony. That she was staying with relatives in Europe. I wondered how long he would be able to get away with that story. Maybe he was just buying some more time.

I was leaning against a tree. My eyes hidden behind black-framed Ray Bans. My shirt drenched from perspiration beneath my new navy blazer. Adam was standing on the other side of the tree. His forehead was beaded with sweat that glistened in the early morning sun. He wore a tight-fitting gray suit, his arms folded. Brown sunglasses kept slipping down his nose. Occasionally he faced me. Just checking me out. Wondering, perhaps, how I was taking it. He knew her death had hit me hard. She was just a kid I told him. A good kid. Probably figured there was more to it than that. Maybe there was. Me and a fifteen-year-old kid. Was it any stranger than Gage and a porno queen?

These were strange times.

After the brief sermon, the crowd dispersed. Gage and the elderly woman were whisked off in a limo.

I waited awhile and wandered over to the site. I watched the workers as they controlled the automatic lift to lower the coffin into the deep hole. Adam put his hand on my shoulder. He asked, "Are you holdin' up okay, buddy?"

"Sure, Adam." I took off my jacket and undid my tie. "It's real muggy."

"Yep." He wiped his brow. "Goddamn summer."

"It's almost over."

"Then we get to freeze our balls off." He quipped under his breath.

"That's New York."

"A helluva town."

I smiled and gave Adam the eye. "Anything yet on Savage?"

"Not much. She's clean."

"You mean she never solicited . . . shot up . . . *any*thing?"

"No record." He said. "A clean bill of health."

"Not even a social disease?" I joked.

"I have her address . . . " He reached into his pocket and took out a piece of paper.

"An uptown girl?" I asked.

"Nope. Downtown. A renovated loft in Tribeca." He handed me the address.

"No Man's Land." I commented.

"Prime real estate these days."

"Make a nice hiding place maybe."

"For a rendezvous with Gage?" He arched his eyebrows.

"Why not?" I smirked.

Adam shrugged. "How're you goin' to handle it?"

"Round-the-clock surveillance." I declared flatly.

"That could be pretty boring."

"With a porno queen? I don't know about that." I jested.

"She's also renting a summer house." Adam added.

"Oh yeah?"

"In Amagansett."

"Why that's convenient." Amagansett was just a hop-and-a-skip from Gage's house.

"Another thing I found interesting." Adam said as we started to walk off.

"What's that?"

"Sam Rayburn."

I stopped in my tracks and faced Adam. "The owner of RayBeam Video, what about him?"

"He lives out there, too." Adam whipped out his note pad. "A house on Cranberry Hole Road. You know where that is?"

"Sure do . . . Promised Land." I related. "Pretty secluded area. Bunch of old deserted fish factories out there."

"Well, that fits with his lifestyle." Adam walked on.

"I figured him for a tropical island myself." I trailed after him.

Adam shrugged. "I found it queer for them all to be livin' out there together. Makes you wonder."

"Adam, this whole case makes me wonder." I said.

I sat outside Zoe Savage's building in my beat-up Porsche. It was times like this that I wished I had never given up smoking. A luke-warm bottle of Amstel Light was tucked between my legs. I was halfway through a porn rag that featured an exclusive interview with Miss Savage herself. And plenty of full color spreads as well. She was quite a knockout in a sleazy sort of way. She had a down-turned mouth that gave her a naturally childish pout. The interview itself wasn't much. She just dropped a lot of smutty talk. Spoke of her Kansas upbringing with a preacher father and drunken mother. The usual bullshit. She sounded like she memorized a character from some bad novel she had read as a kid. She didn't mention any boyfriends. And her most challenging role had been to play against a transsexual that had tits *and* a boner! I was sorry I missed that one.

At one point I got out of the car and dumped the mag in a trash can. I just couldn't stand to look at it anymore. I returned to the car and opened up another warm beer. It was near dusk and I suspected she probably only came out at night.

I had hoped that she and Gage would get together. But he might be afraid now with all the media attention he was getting. They might have to cool it for a while. That would be a bummer for me. I was count-ing on him being horny and in need of some release after playing the grief-stricken daddy for a few days.

I watched the arms of my chronograph turn slowly through the night. I got out of the car a dozen times to stretch my legs. There wasn't much activity down here at this time. She disappointed me. I had figured her to be a nocturnal swinger. Maybe she was in hid-ing. Finally, I decided to check out the building.

I crossed the street and entered the small, cramped vestibule. There was no doorman. The inner door was locked. A video camera was secured at one corner of the ceiling. Ring the bell and the tenant can see you but you can't see her. The door was glass and fitted with a bolt lock. Not too secure there. Maybe it was wired for an alarm. There were no names on the buzzers. Just apartment numbers.

I returned to my car. I couldn't imagine sitting here much longer. What should I do?

I was reminded of the stake out in front of a Harlem tenement building awaiting the Dagger Intruder. I had spent weeks on end waiting for something to happen. For my suspect to make his move. Soon after his last attack, the police had picked up a suspect. His name was Grant Thomas. He had a track record going back to childhood. He had started out with petty crimes that later mushroomed to assaults with a deadly weapon. Mostly knives. And most interesting of all, his last arrest had him sticking an ice pick in his father's leg during a heated argument. He had spent half of his twenty-eight years in detention centers, halfway houses, and jail. After a few days, he had been released on bail. I had been tailing him ever since.

But nothing had been happening. He had been playing it cool. . . .

One night, Matrix joined me. It was mid-February and there was a blanket of snow all around us.

"There's gotta be a better way." Matrix complained.

"Patience, kid, patience."

"We know it's him, so why bother, man?" He asked.

"We have to catch him in the act. Otherwise he'll get off for lack of evidence—believe me." I related.

Matrix shook his head. "We got a set of prints . . . we have witnesses."

I shook my head. "You ain't got shit, kid. I've seen this crap before. They nab the guy and he gets off on a technicality."

"Well, that's the law—people do have rights, y'know."

"Scum like this doesn't deserve rights. He's an animal."

"Well, he isn't going to make a move now. He would be an asshole to do anything at this time." Matrix reasoned.

I faced him. "He's sick. He's a pervert. He gets urges . . . uncontrollable urges. He can't suppress it for too long . . . he'll need a fix soon enough."

Matrix sized me up. "You sure sound like you know how a mind like that ticks."

I smirked. "What's the matter, kid, afraid I'm a loon, too?"

He didn't answer me. He didn't have to. I knew how he felt.

"Well, I'm calling it a night." He opened the car door, the interior light pouring down on us.

I snatched his arm. "Don't worry, I'll deliver him in gift-wrapping."

Matrix looked me in the eye nervously and asked, "Will he still be breathing, Mitch?"

The kid knew what I had in mind.

I snapped out of my musings and scanned my watch. It was after three. I started the engine and drove back to my apartment. I'd try again tomorrow.

When I returned home, I found Jesse sound asleep. I gave her a peck on her forehead and got in next to her. It felt good to be back in the sack. My body ached with stiff muscles. I couldn't wait to get back to my house and start working out again. That always made me feel better.

I closed my eyes and tried to clear my head. But I had Zoe Savage on my mind. I knew that she was my ticket to Gage. I had to get to him through her. I

knew Pike wouldn't be far behind. Then I keyed in
on Rayburn. Where did he fit into this puzzle? Was
he the mastermind in this whole affair? Rumor had it
he was completely out of his mind. His wife and
children long gone. A man in his mid-forties who
had burned out early. Too much, too soon. The old
Hollywood formula.

And then there was Montana. He was on the side-
lines taking it all in. A spectator? Or something
more? Maybe Rayburn was the coach calling the
shots. Gage was the quarterback. Pike was the receiver running the distance. I was the defensive tackle.

But I was the only member on my team. How
could I hold my own against such a powerful oppos-
ing team?

I fell asleep before I could figure it out.

21

CUTTING LOOSE

KATE DIDN'T HAVE A FACE

anymore. She looked like a mannequin or a George Segal sculpture. A little blurry but very real. She was in the bathtub. She loved taking baths. I had just come in from work. My clothes were soiled and reeked from the street. I was working undercover as a druggie, wandering among the scum in lower Manhattan. I stood over her. The water was gray, no suds, her plump breasts bobbing on the surface. Since she no longer possessed a face I could not see her expression. But I felt it. It was one of repulsion.

I stripped off my rank clothes and stood before her naked. When I stepped into the warm water, she sprang up. We stood facing one another. Her face was still unclear. I brought my mouth to her's. I recoiled when a sharp cold sensation burned my lips. I heard her laughter echoing inside my eardrums. Her skin bleached white before my eyes. She appeared as she had at the morgue, her carcass drained of blood. And then I felt her icy hands on me, pulling me closer to her, our bodies now touching. She pushed her lips to mine, her abnormally long tongue probing the inner recesses of my mouth, slinking down my throat like a venomous snake. My body began to glow as it slowly fused into hers. Our two bodies became one brilliant white entity. It was then that I saw her face . . . the face of death. A maggot-ridden skull, the eyeballs still intact . . . staring . . .

A blank stare. An accusing gaze. One that seized me, made my heart pound in my chest.

Suddenly I felt someone shaking me. I rolled over and peeled back my eyelids. It was Jesse. My body was soaked with perspiration, my heart still hammering in my breast. It took a few seconds for me to focus. She was wearing her robe. That meant there was company. I sat up and rubbed the sand from my eyes.

"Adam's here." She said, then noticing my disorientation, added: "Are you okay?"

"I'm fine." I put my feet on the cold floor. "What's this about Adam?"

"He says it's important."

I got up and followed her out to the kitchen. I was wearing only my briefs.

Adam was at the table sipping a cup of coffee. He stood up when I came into the room. A concerned Jesse stood by the fridge. Her arms wrapped tightly around her.

"Mornin' Adam." I poured myself a cup of coffee while I raked my fingers through my disheveled hair.

"I'm afraid it's bad news, Mitch."

I squinted at him confoundedly.

Adam said, "I have a warrant for your arrest."

Jesse brought a hand to her mouth to stifle an outburst.

"What?" I took him in perplexingly. "Are you serious?"

"I'm sorry, Mitch. It's Romanus' collar but I volunteered to do the dirty work." He related.

"What a pal!" I sneered.

"I have to read you your rights." He said then proceeded to read them off a card.

Jesse came up to me. "Mitch—what does this mean?"

"I'm a murderer now. I guess Gage scored a touchdown." I retorted nastily.

She didn't find my crack very amusing. "What should I do?"

"I don't know." I shrugged my shoulders. "I really don't know." I turned and started back to the bedroom. "I'll go get dressed."

I heard their voices in the kitchen. Jesse was giving Adam a hard time. Poor kid. All this was happening much too fast for her. Me? I can't say I was surprised. More angry really. Now I owed Romanus one.

I put on a pair of jeans, a short-sleeved powder blue dress shirt and my new blazer. No tie. A pair of black Reeboks. Then I stuck my head into a sink full of water and combed back my wet hair. The heat outside would dry it soon enough.

I rejoined them in the kitchen. Jesse was in tears. If Adam could blush he would have been beet red by this time. She had really torn into him. He looked more upset than me.

"Let's get this over with." I said.

Jesse rushed up and embraced me.

"Don't worry, Jess, they don't have capital punishment in this state." I quipped.

Adam glared at me angrily.

"Don't take it so hard, Adam. I'll get out of this." I remarked.

He nodded.

I kissed Jesse. "Call my lawyer, babe."

"How can they do this?" She asked in dismay.

"When they have nothing else to go on . . ."

"Come on, Mitch." Adam took hold of my arm and escorted me out the door.

While we waited in the hallway for the elevator, Adam turned to me and said: "You know, Mitch, you're a real prick sometimes."

I grinned.

"Poor Jesse was upset enough without your wise ass comments."

I raised my hands. "Aren't you going to cuff me?"

"I don't have to worry about you running off on me do I?" Adam asked with raised eyebrows.

"Never can tell." I smirked.

He gave me the once over. "Are you packin'?"

"Never can tell . . ." I repeated in a singsong voice.

"You better cut out the cute stuff, Mitch. Romanus will burn you alive."

"Y'know Adam, you sound more and more chicken shit everyday." I told him.

The doors opened and we entered the elevator. I pressed the "L" button.

"Why're you actin' like this?" Adam asked with concern.

"Acting like what?"

He grabbed hold of me and threw me up against the wall. "DON'T FUCK WITH ME, MITCH!"

I shoved him away. "Hands off!"

He stuck his big fat finger in my face. "Wise up! This is a serious situation!"

After a few beats of calmness, I said, "I guess the photos from the video didn't work."

"Guess not." He cooled down and adjusted his clothes.

I patted him on the back. "I'm sorry, man. Just trying to deal with it."

"You sure have a funny way of dealin' with it."

The doors opened and we walked through the lobby, past the doorman, and into the sticky gray air.

It was then that the two men took us from both sides. One stood to Adam's right, hand in jacket pocket. The other put his arm around me. He whispered into my ear, "This way. Mr. Mitchum."

Adam said, "What the hell?"

The man to his right put his arm around him, the hand in his pocket up against Adam's gut. "Chill out, big guy, I have a gun."

I looked to my captor for an explanation. He said, "Mr. Montana's waiting for you."

I looked back at Adam. He was being escorted down the street.

"Don't worry, nothing will happen to your friend if he behaves himself."

I got into the rear seat of a green Buick and the car took off.

The driver craned his head around to take me in. Then he put his eyes back on the road.

I faced my captor who sat next to me. He was a well-groomed young man with an olive complexion. He was wearing a black suit.

We pulled up beside Montana's stretch Mercedes and the chauffeur opened my door.

"Have a nice day." My captor smiled.

I went from the green Buick to the limo where I joined Montana in the back seat.

"Good morning, Mr. Mitchum." Montana flashed his contagious smile.

My head was still spinning. "What just happened?"

"You narrowly escaped, my friend."

"Isn't that breaking the law?"

He laughed. "You have a wonderful sense of humor, Mitch."

"I'm serious. This will only make it tougher for me."

"Tougher than being tucked away behind bars? I hardly think so. Do you have any idea what they do to cops in prison?" He asked, his eyes twinkling from the thought.

I gulped. "Never gave that much thought."

"Besides, as soon as you uncover the truth, all will be forgiven."

"Can I get that in writing?" I quipped.

Montana laughed again.

"There's going to be a manhunt out for me. I am a murder suspect y'know."

"Yes." He faced me and studied my features. "A beard and hair dye might help."

"Sounds like my old days as an undercover cop."

"There is a cyclical pattern in life isn't there?" Montana asked knowingly.

I glanced out the window and watched the buildings sweep by. "Where are we going?"

"I know someone who could do your face over. That should make it a little more difficult for the authorities."

"Then what?"

"Then you'll drive out to the Hamptons." Montana retorted.

"Is that wise?" I inquired.

"It's the only way. Everybody's out there."

"Who's everybody?"

Montana pursed his lips, waiting a few seconds before he answered. "All the players."

"Zoe Savage?"

"She's at her summer rental. I guess I should've told you that yesterday. Would've saved you all that time wasted outside her Manhattan apartment."

I eyed him. "Maybe you should fill me in on what else you know, Mr. Montana?" I was too irate to ask him pleasantly.

He smiled. "In due time."

He was beginning to get on my nerves with his noble attitude. "What is this—a game to you? My fucking ass is on the line! I don't like that. And I don't like what I'm thinking about you, Montana."

He gave me an icy look. "Don't overstep your boundaries, Mitch. You're in no position to take me on. Do we understand one another?"

"How is it I have the feeling you know more about this than you're letting on?"

"You're right. This is a game. A game of chess.

And you happen to be my game piece. My knight. I have Gage in check. And you . . . you're going to finish the game. Win it for me. Checkmate.'' Montana revealed.

"I should tear your fucking head off!" I said through clenched teeth.

Montana shook his head. "Don't worry, I'll take care of you."

And then it hit me. It was like someone had opened a door that lead to my brain, a light illuminating the darkness. "It was you who started this . . . this game. Wasn't it? You had poor Wesen give me that goddamn video tape. You got the ball rolling. Why?"

Montana faced me, his eyes burning into me. "To flush them out."

"And why me?"

"You were experienced. An ex-cop. I figured you could handle yourself. I didn't want Gage to suspect I was involved."

"You bastard. What about the murders?" I asked.

He shook his head. "I have no ideas about that. Gage must be up to something." He glanced my way. "Maybe he saw a sucker. Kill off his family, tack it onto you. He ends up cleaning up his whole mess and getting the girl at the end as well." He was almost gloating from the thought. Probably respecting Gage's ingenuity.

"Nice people." I commented.

"I'm sorry I couldn't tell you sooner. But I had to make sure I could trust you." Montana added.

"Why tell me now?"

"I figured I owe you that much. You've been put through a lot. I understand that. You'll be compensated. Just think, you'll get a sparkling new shop out of it." He offered.

I thought about wrapping my hands around his throat. But what good would that do me? Romanus would only hang another murder rap on me. "What about Romanus?"

He smiled again.

"Is he on your payroll too?" I inquired curiously.

"Romanus?" He grinned sardonically. "Why he's the most honest cop I know."

"I don't believe this. Who else is on your payroll— what about Adam?"

"Your buddy—no, he's clean." He related.

I wondered about that. He was the one who had set things up for me with Montana. "Don't you even care what this is doing to me? My personal life? My reputation?"

"Everything would've been settled very quietly if it wasn't for the murders. They weren't in my game plan." Montana admitted.

I shook my head. "If I ever get out of this . . ."

"Don't worry, you will. That much I can promise you."

"Then you better hire yourself a bodyguard." I threatened.

He seemed amused. "You certainly are from the old school, Mitch."

"Don't I frighten you? I'm a desperate man." I emphasized.

He faced me. "You're too much."

"What if I turn the tables on you, Montana. What if I start playing ball with Gage? Maybe I already have." I led him on.

"If you had you wouldn't be here, my friend. In fact, you wouldn't even be breathing." He declared sternly.

I nodded. He was right. I had to go along for the ride, to see this through to the bitter end.

"Don't despair. Things will work out for you. After this, you'll never have to deal with me ever again."

I said, "Promises, promises."

22

MIRROR, MIRROR

I GAZED UPON my reflection in
the mirror and saw someone else. My hair was dark-
ened on top—my temples gray. I had a full salt-
and-pepper beard and wore tortoise-shell framed
glasses. Dressed in a white shirt, jeans, and light-
weight tweed blazer, I looked exactly like a college
professor.

Montana and the make-up artist stood behind me.
We were in the back room of a chic hair salon on
West Fifty-seventh Street.

I swung around. "I don't fucking believe it."

"A whole new man!" The woman quipped.

Montana came up to me and adjusted my jacket.
"Not bad, Mitchum."

"But will I fool anybody?"

"And how!" The make-up artist exclaimed.

"That'll be all." Montana dismissed the woman.

After she left, he took me in again. Sized me up.
The gears turning inside his head. "Well, what do
you think?"

"I think . . . I think this just might work." I said.

He handed me a piece of paper. ''Those are Savage's and Rayburn's addresses.''

I read them. I knew the areas well. There would be no problem.

''And these.'' He handed me a key ring.

I recognized the car keys immediately. A Porsche. ''What are these?'' I shook them.

''Keys to your new set of wheels. You like sports cars—yes?'' Montana smirked.

''A Porsche?''

''A Nine Twenty-eight Turbo.'' He retorted.

I whistled. It wasn't everyday some dude gave you the keys to a forty-five thousand dollar automobile. ''Do I look like the kind of man who drives around in sports cars?''

''I felt the Porsche would be less conspicuous in the Hamptons than a Honda.'' He jested.

''Too bad this is only make-believe.'' I uttered under my breath.

''And you'll need this.'' He whipped out a Browning nine millimeter automatic pistol with suppressor.

I held the blue-black weapon in my hand and snapped in a cartridge. ''Don't you know silencers are against the law?'' I joked.

''It might just come in handy.'' He winked.

And then it dawned on me.

A gun with a silencer.

That only meant one thing.

A hit!

''Whaddaya planning on, Montana? Is this for self-defense or have I become your shooter?'' I inquired suspiciously.

He wiped the smile from his face and cocked his

head to one side. "I think you might consider it self-preservation."

"I'm not going to do your dirty work for you, Montana. I'm not one of your hired guns." I snapped.

"Have I said anything about whacking anyone?" Montana asked innocently.

"Guns speak louder than words." I held up the pistol.

"You're in a great deal of trouble. People are coming after you. They'll have guns."

"And maybe all the right people will get shot while I'm busy protecting myself." I quipped.

He smirked. "Perhaps."

"No way, pal!" I pitched the gun into a dry sink that rang out with a metal-on-metal clank.

"Don't be foolish, Mitchum. What choice have you got?"

"One murder hanging over my head is enough, thank you."

"I told you. You don't have to worry about the murder rap." He assured me.

"No, you'll just snap your fingers and make it all go away." I said sarcastically.

"Something like that." Montana remarked confidently.

I scrutinized him. "How far do your tentacles reach, Montana?"

"Farther than you would ever dream possible." He related.

I nodded. "Yeah, I can believe that."

He picked up the Browning and gave it to me. "You don't have to do any shooting if you don't want to."

I smiled. ''Only, of course, if somebody's shooting at me.''

He said, ''Of course.''

I stopped off at a Howard Johnson's along the way. I had a cup of coffee before I made a phone call to Adam. I was wondering how he made out after our little incident this morning.

''Hello, Adam?''

''WHERE THE FUCK ARE YOU?!'' He shouted into the phone.

''I'm safe.''

''Damn—did you set that up?'' He asked furiously.

''Hell no. I didn't know you were coming to arrest me.''

''Then who was behind it?'' He demanded to know.

''Who else—Montana.'' I replied.

''Natch. And who tipped him off?''

''Montana knew about it before you did.'' I related.

''Whaddaya sayin'?''

''I'm saying he probably gave the word to have me picked up.'' I informed him.

''WHAT?!'' Adam shrieked.

''You're not on his payroll—are you, Adam?''

''I'm goin' to kick your ass the next time I see you! *On his payroll*. Bullshit. I'm on nobody's payroll.'' Adam contended.

''Well, I wish I could say the same about Romanus.'' I added.

''Romanus? I don't believe it!'' Adam exclaimed.

''Well, start believing it, pal. Montana has been

pulling the strings all along on this. He just came clean with me.''

''Why would he come clean now?''

''Because it's time to wrap this one up.'' I asserted.

''You better getcha ass in here and fast.'' Adam wasn't going to have any of this.

''Romanus a little peeved, is he?'' I asked mockingly.

''He thinks I helped you get away.''

''Did they print up wanted posters of me yet?'' I laughed.

''I swear I'm goin' to take you apart, Mitch!'' Adam was still fuming.

''Take it easy, Adam. Something's about to come down soon. Everything will be cool.'' I assured him.

''There's been another development in the case.'' Adam related with a heavy sigh that seemed to ease his fury.

''Oh?''

''I shouldn't be tellin' you this.'' He lowered his voice.

''Oh, come on, Adam. You can't get into any more trouble than you're already in.'' I teased him.

''Gee, thanks.'' He said, then added: ''Another witness has come forward.''

''Oh yeah? Go on.'' I urged him.

''She says she saw a woman with Chloe just before you came around.''

''A woman?'' I asked. ''What did she look like?''

''I was just comin' to that. She had long dark hair.''

''Yeah . . .''

"She was sitting next to the girl on the bench. And
. . . now this is the important part . . ."

"I'm all ears, Adam." I was getting annoyed at
him for dragging this out.

"This woman . . . she had on a pair of those Yoko
Ono shades. That was how the witness described
them. Those Porsche sun shields."

"You're kidding?"

"Nope. That made Romanus go back to your pho-
tos from the video. He showed them to the woman.
She said it sure looked like the person she saw."
Adam conveyed.

"That puts me in the clear." I said with relief.

"Well, Romanus still needs to talk with you fur-
ther. That's why you have to haul your ass in here."

I thought about it. It meant that I was no longer a
suspect. But it still left some important questions
unanswered. Like who was the real killer? I decided to
follow through on my plans. I had more of a chance
to uncover the truth than Romanus did at this point. I
said, "I'm too close to throw in the towel now,
Adam. I have one more shot and I'm going for it."

"Mitch."

"Take care of Jesse for me. Tell her I'm alright.
And for chrissakes keep her there in Manhattan until
all this blows over."

"Mitch!" Adam screeched.

I hung up.

I went outside and got into my shining red Porsche.
The sun was setting. It had been a long day and I still
had a good hour's drive ahead of me. The engine
turned over like a purring lion. I revved it up. Feeling the powerful engine beneath me.

I got back on the L.I.E. heading east to the Hamptons.

The Hamptons.

Where it had all started.

Where it had to end.

23

SAVAGE GRACE

I SPENT THE NIGHT in a small motel along Route 27 in Amagansett. Of course, I could not spend the night at my home. I was sure the local authorities had it staked out. It was unusual to find a vacancy during the summer season, but the tourist trade had been slow. With the strong dollar, vacationers had flocked to Europe instead. Also with more and more condo developments bringing in year-round residents, the Hamptons were eclipsing their resort area image. While businesses catering to tourists were hurting, the businesses dealing with essentials like food and, yes, video flourished. Residents bought their food in supermarkets and cooked at home capping off the evening with a video tape.

Another problem was the weather. The summer had been hot, muggy, and very wet. It rained most weekends. This only dampened local spirit more.

I'm afraid my sleep brought on more reruns from Kate's murder investigation. I was staking out Grant Thomas, the suspected Dagger Intruder. It was a brisk frosty evening when he made his inevitable

213

move. I only wished that Matrix had been there to assist me . . . to restrain me. I got out of my car and trailed after him. He was dressed in a peacoat with a long brown knit scarf. A blue knit cap was pulled over his short afro. A tall man, his giraffe-like legs carried him swiftly to the subway station. I continued my pursuit, staying back as far as I could to avoid detection.

He waited on the platform for the train to pull in. He wrapped his arms around himself and shuffled his feet to stay warm. I hid behind a support column. I scanned my watch: 11:45 PM. I heard the metal screeching of an oncoming train.

It whisked into the station with a burst of heated air that blew Thomas' scarf behind him like a wagging flag. After he boarded, I slipped into the car in front of his. I walked to the back of the car and stood there, my eyes peering through the windows of the doors that separated us. He was sitting nonchalantly on a deserted bank of seats.

And there I stayed for almost three-quarters of an hour until Thomas stood up and exited at the Fourteenth Street station. He was back in familiar territory. His crimes were all committed below Fourteenth Street—far from his Harlem home turf.

I followed after him, keeping my distance. He walked purposefully. Like he knew where he was going . . . like he had it all mapped out beforehand. Had he planned it right before his abrupt arrest or was he about to improvise?

He ventured eastward. The streets were dark and desolate, an eerie silence hung in the frigid air. There was a zigzag pattern to his journey, as though he wanted to make sure nobody could retrace his steps.

It was when he got to the Lower East Side that I decided he really did have a place in mind. Yes, our man had already done his homework weeks before. He slunk into the murky alleyway between two tenement buildings and disappeared into the darkness.

I entered the dank alley after him. It was so dark I couldn't see my hand in front of my face. I inched along, my hands groping the brick walls on either side of me. The alley led to an opening to the buildings' backyards. I scanned the area, then shifted my gaze to the fire escapes in the back of the buildings. I spotted Thomas as he slowly trekked up the rusty steps, stopping at the top floor landing.

I observed him in the moonlight as he removed his coat and spread it out on the fire escape. His coat was probably lined with pockets that held his tools.

I climbed the ladder of the fire escape and began my ascent. He had already jimmied open the window by the time I reached the story beneath him. He slipped silently inside.

I hauled out my gun and went up to the next flight. I saw the flicker of his penlight inside the dark apartment. I stepped through the open window, my gun at the ready. With a quick scan I found myself in the person's living room. It was then I heard the yelp. It sounded from the other room. A woman's distress call. I froze as I listened to the hushed murmuring coming from the adjacent room . . . most likely the bedroom. Another yelp then a slap. I heard a loud thump and a breathy man's voice say, ''SHUT UP OR I'LL CUT YOU!''

I carefully worked my way towards the voices. I came out into the kitchen, then headed to the open door.

I found him on the floor, his trousers bundled at his ankles, his shiny black ass gyrating in the night air. He was pumping a dark-haired woman who lay face-down on the wooden floor. She sobbed loudly, her nightgown pushed up on her back. Thomas held a dagger at her throat.

I switched on the overhead light and broke into the combat position. "FREEZE!"

Thomas gazed up at me with popping eyes. Saliva, like a silver thread, oozed from his mouth to the woman's squirming face. His ass stopped moving. "WHAT THE FUCK?!" He hissed.

"GET UP!" I commanded.

"I'll cut her throat!" He threatened.

"Go ahead, give me an excuse to blow your head off, boy." I sneered.

He gulped loudly then dropped the knife. He stood up on his knees, his glistening black member hanging limply between his legs.

"Put your pants on!" I told him.

He stood up and wiggled into his tight jeans. His eyes never left me. "You a cop?"

"You'll wish that I was."

The Hispanic woman continued to lay face down on the floor, her moans growing uncontrollably louder. Her bare buttocks were red from his brutal attack, her panties were stuffed in her mouth.

"You're not a cop?" He asked, confounded by my intrusion.

A smile spread across my face. "No, I'm the Angel of Death, asshole . . ."

I shot up in bed. My face was beaded with sweat. I kicked off the sheets and lay back in bed. I tasted bile in the back of my throat. I heard nothing but the hum of the air conditioner and the distant traffic noise from the main roadway.

I felt for my watch in the darkness. The fluorescent numbers glowed six a.m. I got out of bed and went to the window, pulling open the drapes. A flood of sunshine poured into the dank room. After my eyes adjusted, I spotted the empty pint bottle of Jack Daniel's that lay on it's side on the bedside table.

I hurried into the bathroom in time to drop to my knees and retch into the toilet bowl. Nothing solid came up. I sat down on the cold tile floor and held my stomach, my nostrils resisting the stench of the invisible vomit.

After an invigorating early morning swim in the motel's pool, I had breakfast at a local restaurant. Then I took a drive out to Savage's place. A small driftwood A-frame on a private road just off Montauk Highway, it was situated in an overcrowded development along Marine Boulevard near the Napeague Strip. The community was a smorgasbord of different style beach houses and chalets clustered together. I could never understand its appeal. You had virtually no privacy or property. It's only selling point was the walking distance to the surf.

I had difficulty finding the house at first. It was like looking for a needle in a haystack. But after figuring out the logistics of the area, I discovered it nestled between a large post-modern architectural showplace and a prefabricated chalet.

There was a yellow Corvette parked in front with a faded Mondale/Ferraro bumper sticker on it. I went up the steps to the deck and found her stretched out on a wooden chaise wearing red-framed Wayfarer sunglasses and not much else. Her white knit bikini top was pulled down beneath her bulging bust, her brown nipples peeking out. Her bronzed body greased down. A tall glass of iced coffee stood at arm's reach on a table next to her. She wasn't aware of my presence which meant either her eyes were closed or she was taking a snooze.

She didn't look like the same Zoe Savage I had seen on the big screen. Her brown hair was lighter, her bod less fleshy. I took her in, from her pretty head down to her long shapely legs and painted toenails. Here I was standing inches away from a porn queen. I could feel the strong reaction down below.

I don't know how long I stood there staring like a gaping teenager. I hadn't had an experience like it since I was a voyeur in the girls' locker room in high school.

But all good things had to come to an end. So I said, "Morning, Ms. Savage."

She turned her head and gave me the once-over with her chocolate brown orbs peeking above the frames of her shades. "Yes?" Her voice was sleepy and sexy and I think I had a crush.

"Mr. Gage sent me."

"Brandon?" She sat up and put her feet on the deck. "He didn't say anything to me about this."

"It was kind of sudden. The name's Pike." I put out my hand for her.

She squinted up at me, the skin around her eyes crinkling like an accordion. She wasn't as young as I thought. She took hold of my hand and pushed herself up on her feet. She whipped her sunglasses off and reinforced her bikini top.

I followed her into the house. It was decorated with standard beach house wicker furniture, a fireplace in the center of the sunken living room. It had high cathedral ceilings and a bedroom loft. The whole place smelled like Coppertone. She went to the small kitchen and sat on a stool before the breakfast bar. A half-eaten croissant was sitting on a gray plate. She picked up a cordless phone and started to punch the keys.

I snatched the phone out of her hands. "Whaddaya doing Ms. Savage?"

"I'm calling Brandon." She had a hard look on her face.

"I wouldn't disturb him right now." I said pleasantly.

"Why did he send you?"

"For protection." I replied.

She squinted at me again. She should really watch that. Crow's feet on a porn actress could blow it for me. She asked, "From what?"

"That Mitchum guy—he escaped from police custody." I related.

"Shit." She snapped. "This whole thing's getting out of hand."

"I'll say." I put the phone back on its cradle and picked up the croissant. "You mind?"

She shook her head.

I put the whole thing in my mouth. The flaky bread melted on my tongue. She cocked her head to one side and said, "You don't look like the man Brandon described."

"Is that a fact?"

"Yeah, he said you were an old-timer." She said.

I brushed back my graying hair. "Well, I'm not a youngster anymore."

"And you don't look much like an ex-con, either." She rubbed her chin.

"What's an ex-con supposed to look like?"

She said, "Not like you."

I grinned. "You've seen too many movies, Ms. Savage."

She smiled at that. "Maybe I've *appeared* in too many."

"That's right, you're an . . . actress." I said.

"You don't have to be polite around me, Mr. Pike. I'm a porno star."

"Yeah, I've seen your work—you're good." I dropped my head in embarrassment. "Not that I go to many of those. Y'know. Ever think about going legit?" I inquired, having a difficult time refraining from laughing.

She shrugged.

"Yah never know."

"I'm thinking about it." She admitted coyly.

The more I looked at her, the more I could see her in a rain slicker and Porsche Design sport sunglasses. Why not? Kill off the competition to keep Brandon

Gage all for herself. It wouldn't be the first time a mistress had tried it. "You should really consider it, Ms. Savage."

"Brandon is working on it."

"I would think Rayburn could help." I threw his name out.

She laughed. "Rayburn? Ha! His name's poison in Hollywood."

"Doesn't he run RayBeam Video?" I questioned dumbly.

She screwed her mouth up mockingly. "Brandon runs RayBeam."

"Oh? I don't know how those things work." I said.

She hopped off the stool. "Can I get you something . . . to drink?"

"Some of that iced coffee would be fine."

She went to the counter to prepare it. "I just find it strange that Brandon didn't tell me about you last night."

"Just found out about Mitchum this morning."

"Brandon up first thing in the morning?" She howled at the idea. "Not the man I know."

"Well, he received a phone call."

She returned with my drink. "Milk and sugar?"

I nodded.

She mixed them in. "I hear you're from Boston . . . I don't detect an accent."

"I'm not a local . . . just been living up there for the past few years."

She handed me the cold glass. I took a sip. "Thank you."

She sat down again, her eyes never leaving me.

I scratched my beard. The spirit gum was driving me crazy.

"You have that long?" She asked.

"What's that?"

"Your beard—you keep scratching it."

"Yeah, it's pretty recent. Thought it would give me a different look." I grinned.

"It's very distinguished on you. Always wanted Brandon to grow one. He used to have a mustache, y'know."

"Yeah, I could see him with a mustache."

She put on that hard face again. "His wife made him shave it off."

"Well, I guess he doesn't have to worry about his wife anymore."

"Yeah, that's right." She softened up.

"Too bad about his kid, though."

She shrugged. "She was a little brat. Had her daddy wrapped around her little finger—y'know what I mean?"

I nodded. My little love goddess here had a cold heart. "Kind of makes it a clear path for you, huh?" I tossed her a sly wink.

She nodded in deep thought. I would've done anything to crack open that skull and find out what was going on inside.

"I heard the police aren't all that convinced that Mitchum's the guilty party. Seems there's a woman involved." I informed her.

"A woman?"

"Yeah." I said, adding: "Or a man disguised as one."

"Brandon didn't mention anything about that."

"You two don't seem to communicate too well." I uttered.

She didn't like hearing that from me and gave me a dirty look.

"Sure makes it interesting, though." I continued. "Wonder what else Gage has been keeping to himself?"

"Whaddaya mean by that?" She asked accusingly.

"Just making small talk. I mean, I always felt he was holding back on me. He never gave me the whole dope. Like . . . what is he really up to?"

"He must have his reasons for keeping you in the dark."

"But he seems to be holding back with you, too." I remarked.

"I don't like this conversation." She stood up and tramped into the living room.

I trailed after her with my glass in hand. She plopped down on the cushioned wicker sofa and picked up a leftover section from the Sunday *Newsday*. I sat down on an adjacent chair. I looked over her Sansui stereo rack system and small Sony color set. An early model RCA video recorder was on the floor, the electrical cord tied around it.

"Your VCR out of commission?"

She rattled the newspaper and uttered something inaudible.

"I apologize if I said something to upset you."

She put down the paper. Her brown eyes burning into me. "I'm tired of listening to your voice, Pike."

"Sorry."

"Just shut up—okay?"

"I didn't realize I hit a sore spot." I persisted.

She took in a deep breath. "How long do you intend to hang out here?"

"Until Mr. Gage tells me otherwise." I replied.

"Well, if I have anything to do with it—that'll be real soon." She shot up and hurried to the phone.

She had almost finished dialing by the time I caught up with her. I grabbed the phone and smashed it against the table. The plastic casing shattered into a zillion pieces. She recoiled from me in horror.

I pulled out my gun and rested it's long barrel and silencer against my shoulder. "Now let's not have any more games, Ms. Savage."

She stepped back until she hit the wall, pressing against it tightly.

I took her hand and peeled her off the wall and walked her back into the living room. "Sit."

She eased onto the sofa, her arms wrapped around her torso.

"Like I said, it's too bad Gage didn't fill you in on everything."

She shook her head in disbelief. "Brandon wouldn't do this."

"Really? Didn't bother him to off his wife and kid." I quipped.

"He had nothing to do with that!"

"He tell you that?" I grinned.

"He . . . he loves me."

"He loved his old lady and kid, too." I snickered.

"Why are you doing this?" She asked.

"I got my orders."

"What orders?"

"Orders from your lover." I said. "Guess he wants to tie up all the loose ends."

"No." She shook her head slowly.

"What did he promise you, honey?"

She was speechless.

"Did he promise to make you a legit star or something? What's the story he gave you?"

"I don't believe this."

"Too real, huh? Not like the movies at all."

"Who are you?" She asked nastily.

"I told you—Hunter Pike. A freelance employee of Brandon Gage. Specialty is arson and elimination. I torched Mitchum's shop and now I eliminate you." I said gleefully.

"You're sick!" She screeched.

"Keep it down, sweetheart."

"I want to talk to Brandon."

"Well, he doesn't want to talk to you."

"He wouldn't do this to me." She declared.

"Naw, he's too nice a guy." I put my foot up on the cocktail table and aimed the gun at her. "Where do you want it?"

She covered her face and began to sob.

I didn't feel too good about what I was doing to this poor girl, but I just had to break her. Get her to go against Gage. That was the only way I could get to him.

"Now, now, now . . ." I said coyly. "Let me see that pretty face of yours."

She put her hands down. Her face was wet with tears. Her eyes black from mascara. She wiped her nose with the back of her hand.

"Listen, I'm really sorry about this. I'm paid to do a job."

"Please . . . I'll do anything." She managed to get out between sobs.

"Anything?" I asked demoniacally.

She nodded her head up and down.

"Hey, that gives me a lot of possibilities." I sat down on the table and aimed the gun away from her.

"I can pay you."

I looked her in the eye and said, "You think I can be bought?"

She swallowed noisily. "I have some money."

"Maybe I don't want money."

She glanced down at herself. "You can have me."

I smirked. "I don't want that either. At least, not like this."

"Then . . . then . . . what do you want?" Her teeth were chattering.

"I want to know the whole scam. I want to know what's coming down. If Gage's involved, we're talking big bucks—am I right?"

She acknowledged me with a nervous nod.

"We're talking about hot videotapes . . . piracy . . . that whole number—right?"

"Uh-huh."

"What else?"

"It's only a short-term thing." She spat out.

"What is?"

"The piracy."

"Why?"

"Brandon . . . he needed to raise a lot of cash."

"For what—he have a cash flow problem or something?"

"It's for an investment." She replied.

"An investment? Honey, you ain't making any sense." I complained.

"He wants to expand the company into original motion picture production."

"Is that where you fit in?" I inquired.

"Yes, he said he would make a Hollywood star out of me. That I had a lot of potential."

"I bet he did!" I tittered.

"He's sincere . . . he loves me." She said, trying to convince herself.

"That's what they all say."

"I believe . . . believed him." She accentuated.

"Is Rayburn involved in this?"

She shook her head. "That's where the money comes in."

"How?"

"Brandon was going to buy the company out from under him. It was all hush-hush. Rayburn wouldn't have known what hit him."

"Nice scheme. With Gage at the helm he could do whatever he wanted, including making a star out of his mistress. But one thing bothers me—why knock off the family?"

"He wasn't involved in that. It was that Mitchum guy. He's a wacko or something."

I laughed.

She stared at me. "What're you going to do now—blackmail Brandon?"

I shook my head.

"You're not really Pike, are you?"

"Nope."

"A cop?"

"No, the name's Mitchum."

Her eyes almost popped out of her head.

"Don't worry. I'm not going to snuff you. In fact, I'm not such a bad guy. Really. I didn't kill Nicola or Chloe." I maintained sincerely.

"Then who did?"

"That's what I want to find out. And I think your boyfriend might be able to help me."

"He didn't do it."

"Maybe . . . maybe not."

"You tricked me . . . now you know everything." She didn't look very happy.

"Well . . . almost."

"What else do you want from me?"

I smiled and said, "I would like you to introduce me to your boyfriend."

24

POINT BLANK

I WATCHED ZOE SAVAGE

get undressed. It was a lot like getting dressed but only backwards. She wasn't too happy about it. She told me I should turn my back. I said it wasn't gentlemanly to turn your back on a woman. So she just shrugged and peeled off her swimsuit and hopped into the shower. I didn't know why she was so modest, I had seen more graphic close-ups of her on the big wide screen.

As she showered, I started to peel off my beard. It was becoming too annoying. I went into the bathroom and rinsed my hair in the sink. It was only vegetable coloring so it washed right out. I finished in time to hand Zoe a towel.

She wrapped herself in it. "So that's what you look like."

"Yep."

"Not bad." She remarked.

"You're not so bad yourself." I winked.

She brushed by me and went into the bedroom to

get dressed. "Brandon's not going to let you get away with this, Mitchum."

"Call me Mitch." I sat down on the edge of the bed. She was pulling a white shirt over her bare torso.

"Do you get off on watching people get dressed?" She inquired nastily.

"Sometimes it's easy on the eyes."

She wiggled into a cotton panty. "What kind of man are you?"

"The horny kind." I admitted.

"Can I ask you something?"

"Sure."

She poured herself into a pair of designer jeans. "You had a chance to take advantage of me back there."

"Still do." I smirked.

"I don't think so."

"I told you I was a swell guy."

"I wouldn't push it if I were you." She tossed back at me.

"Y'know, I think it would've been a lot different if we had met under nicer circumstances." I played it to the hilt.

She said, "Maybe . . . maybe not."

I said, "It's not too late to find out."

She smiled. "With that gun in your hand?"

I looked down at it. "What—does this bother you? Or maybe it turns you on?"

She came closer to me. Her hair still wet from the shower. She was glowing. Her dark nipples showed through her transparent shirt. Her brown eyes on my green eyes. I felt the pressure growing in my loins but I also smelled a rat.

She dropped to her knees and took my face in her hands. She brought her face to mine. Our lips touching. I said, "I wasn't born yesterday, sweetheart." And nudged the gun against her breast.

She stood up and gave me her hard look. The once soft brown eyes now as sharp as razor blades. She sat down before her vanity and began to put on her make-up. Occasionally she would scowl at me. I could feel her animosity.

I wondered how far she would've gone. I wished I could've played along a little longer. It might've gotten interesting.

"How long have you two been at it?" I asked.

She replied with a stern hard face.

"How did you meet?" I persisted.

She dabbed her face furiously with a brush.

"Don't feel much like talking?"

She craned her head around to face me. "I'm afraid your charm escapes me."

"That's too bad. We could've had fun."

"Says you." She hissed.

"I don't know why you're so bent out of shape. I thought we were getting along pretty well. Even on intimate terms."

She shook her head. "You have a real sick sense of humor, y'know that?"

I snickered.

"You really think you have it in the bag, don't you?" She confronted me.

"I'm sitting here holding the gun, sweetheart." I replied confidently.

"We'll see how long that lasts."

"You never know. You might end up seducing me after all."

She finished with her face and stood up, hands on her hips. "Well, I'm ready."

"I'll say!" I tossed her a compliment.

"Where're we going?" She inquired.

"I told you, I wanna meet your boyfriend."

"Whaddaya going to do with him?"

"I wouldn't be so concerned about him, hon. I would mind your own ass if I were you." I conveyed.

"Words of wisdom." She declared sarcastically.

"You know it." I got up and tucked the gun in the back of my pants beneath my jacket. "Let's go."

We took her Corvette. I thought it would be less suspicious if she drove into Gage's driveway. We didn't say much along the way. I could tell she was tense by the white of her knuckles. She gripped the steering wheel for dear life.

She pulled up behind Nicola's red Mercedes.

Nicola.

It seemed like months ago that she'd been murdered.

"You first." I said. "And no funny business."

She got out of the car and walked up the stone foot path to the front door. I hid myself behind a bush.

"Ring the bell." I instructed.

She pressed the doorbell.

I heard the musical chimes.

The door opened and Janet appeared. She held her head up high as she stared down at Zoe. She didn't approve of her one bit.

"Hello, Janet, is Mr. Gage at home?" Zoe asked.

"He's asleep." She replied.

I stepped into the picture and said, "Then let's go wake him up."

I followed the two women through the familiar hallway and towards the closed door at the end of the hall. They paused at the door. I knew where it led—the bedroom. The room where Nicola and I had made love. The room where I had become entangled in a spider's web.

Janet looked to me for instructions.

"Open it." I commanded.

She pushed it opened and we strolled in behind her. A blue silk sheet was draped across Gage. The curtains were drawn, the room in silent darkness. There was a dampness in the room from the overworked central air conditioner.

I drew my gun and advanced to the bed. He was sound asleep. I played with his ear lobe with the barrel of the silencer. He swatted it away as though it were a fly. I stuck the barrel into his ear. His eyes fluttered open.

He groaned when he saw me, the big black gun pressed against him.

"Good morning, Gage." I said sweetly. "Rise and shine."

"You leave him alone!" Zoe wailed.

"Now I want you to sit up . . . very carefully." I stepped back, the gun before me.

He sat up, his eyes scanning the room.

"I'm sorry, Brandon, he threatened me." The actress explained apologetically.

"Who are you?" He asked.

"Oh, come on, Brandon, I'm your friendly local video dealer."

"Mitchum." He deduced.

"The one and only." I announced gleefully.

"I thought they arrested you?"

"Guess again."

"What do you want?" He inquired menacingly.

"I want you."

"Me?"

I nodded, a smile spreading on my face. "Get up."

He pushed away the sheet and got to his feet. He stood there in his blue-striped boxer shorts.

"Nice knees, Brandon." I winked.

He gave Zoe a cold eye.

"He knows everything!" Zoe exclaimed.

"Thanks to your little friend here." I added.

"He threatened me!" Her performance continued.

"Hey, Brandon, she's good. Maybe you were right about making her a legit actress."

He scorched me with his steel-gray eyes. "You're dead, mister."

I took in his hard, chiseled features. The strong jaw line. The deep-set eye sockets. The thick eyebrows. The solid athletic body. He was made of polished stone or marble. A sculptor's ideal model. I placed the gun against his forehead and said, "Don't think so."

"Why are you here?"

"Where's your puppy dog Pike?"

"He's never too far behind." He replied defiantly.

"What makes you think I won't pull the trigger, Gage?"

"I thought ice picks were your specialty, Mitchum."

"Did you really think you'd be able to frame me with that crap, Gage?"

"The police are convinced of it." Gage declared.

"The police have wised up since, Gage."

"Oh?"

"I told them about you, Gage. You're next on their list."

He laughed. "You're really on the edge, son."

I whipped the gun across his face and he fell back on the bed. Zoe ran to him. Blood trickled from his lips.

"Get away from him, Zoe!" I shouted.

She went to stand next to Janet.

Gage wiped his mouth with the back of his hand. His glare blinded me. "You're making a big mistake, Mitchum."

I got up on the bed and sat down on his stomach, my knees on either side of him. The gun against the indentation of his cleft chin. "We'll see who's making the mistake, Gage."

"Leave him alone." Zoe shrieked.

"Shut up!" I bellowed.

Gage just lay there with a bloody smile on his face. I couldn't understand how he could not be threatened by me. Big business must have turned these guys into armor-clad robots.

"Wipe that smile off your face!" I demanded.

"Let's get this over with, Mitchum." He said with a heavy sigh.

"I want to know who killed Nicola and Chloe?"

"You tell me." He retorted with a short cackle.

I brought the handle of the pistol down on his chest. He cringed from the pain and started to cough.

"You had Nicola sleep with me to keep me occupied while Pike torched my shop?"

He nodded and coughed some more.

"Then she was aware of your plans?"

"Yes."

I flashed on Zoe. "Did she know about this one?"

"Of course."

"What kind of people are you?" I asked in disgust.

"Did you tell your girlfriend about sleeping with my wife?" Gage sneered.

I brought the gun down on him again. "Now tell me about the murders."

"Go to hell." He snapped.

"HOLD ON THERE, MITCHUM!" I heard Pike roar.

I looked up and saw him standing between the women, .45 automatic in hand.

"Well, if it isn't our old friend, Hunter Pike." I said.

"Get off him and drop the piece, Mitchum."

"I think I have the advantage here, Pike." I placed the gun between Gage's eyes. "You drop the gun or I blow this sucker's brains out."

"Fat chance." Pike said. "I have two broads here I could send off to the Big Sleep."

"I don't care about them, schmuck." I remarked. "Now drop it!"

Pike studied me for awhile. Then he seized Janet and pressed the gun against her head. "Get off of Mr. Gage."

"Gage, tell your gorilla to drop it."

Gage pulled back his lips to smile.

Pike said, "Enough of this shit." And squeezed the trigger. Janet's head came apart before she even had a chance to scream. Then Pike grabbed Zoe. "She's next."

I looked into Pike's eyes and knew he wasn't fooling around. "You're a fucking maniac!"

"Drop the piece, Mitchum." Pike ordered. He had Zoe in a headlock.

I peered down at Gage. He was still grinning.

I looked up at Zoe. She was crying again. This time she wasn't acting. I tossed my gun to the floor and climbed off Gage.

Gage got to his feet and stood before me. "You're out of your league, Mitchum," he asserted, then punched me in the stomach.

I doubled over and fell to my knees.

Gage said, "Pike—take care of this scumbag for me."

25

KNOCKIN' ON HEAVEN'S DOOR

PIKE ORDERED ME to wrap Janet's body in a plastic shower curtain and clean up the mess. I had difficulty getting the bloodstains out of the bedroom carpet. Although I had seen worse in my time, I never had to wipe it up. It made me very nauseous.

It was nightfall by the time I had finished. Gage came into the bedroom. He stood in the doorway holding a raw filet mignon against his bruised mouth. He gave Pike the eye then set his sights on me. I was sitting on the edge of the bed. I asked, "How're you goin' to explain this one, Gage?"

He shrugged his shoulders dramatically. "People disappear everyday, Mitchum. You, yourself, will find that out shortly." His eyes sparkled.

"This woman has family . . . friends." I continued.

He stood there wearing his white trousers, knit Polo shirt, leather espadrilles and shit-eating grin.

"I don't believe you people." I shook my head in despair.

"For an ex-cop, you're pretty naive." Gage commented.

"You're the second person to tell me that recently. Maybe I am. I guess I'm used to street types. Hardened criminals. I figured intelligent, privileged people would act differently. Now I know better." I declared.

"You're too hung up on morality. If you want to get ahead in this world, you have to eighty-six that ideological crap." Gage contended.

Pike had himself a good laugh over that.

I shifted my gaze to him. He was standing nearby wearing a polyester floral shirt with steel-wool sticking out of the opened collar. "Where does this slug fit in on your evolutionary scale?"

Pike sobered up and advanced towards me, my gun in hand.

"Pike." Gage sang out. "Save it for later."

"Later?" I turned to Gage. "Have big plans for me, do yah?"

He nodded. "It's too bad you had to involve yourself in this."

"Did I have a choice?" I snapped.

"You could've just handed over the tape."

"You burned my shop. You sent this ape after me and my girlfriend. You expected me to just roll over and take it?" I objected.

"It could've stopped at the torch job."

"Yeah—sure. And after you get me out of the way all your problems will be solved."

"Not all of them. But your demise will help make things less complicated." Gage said.

"What about the police?"

"What about them?"

"You think I'm working alone on this?"

He chuckled insincerely. "Now, now . . . Mitchum, let's not start grabbing at straws." He scanned his gold Rolex. "Pike—finish this business." He said, then left the room.

Pike came up to me. "C'mon, Mitchum, on your feet."

He made me carry the body over my shoulder and out to his rented Buick. I dumped it into the trunk. Pike held my gun on me all the while. He told me to get behind the wheel. We were going on a little trip. We were going to visit Nicola.

And then he let out a loud burst of laughter.

That was when I knew I would kill him the first chance I got.

I started the car while he slid in on the passenger side. The long barrel of the silencer stuck in my ribs. I recalled the last time I was in this very same predicament.

I turned to him. "Where to?"

He said, "Get onto Three Mile Harbor Road."

I backed out of the driveway and drove down the street. When we got to the intersection, he said, "Hang a left."

I headed toward town on Three Mile Harbor Road. We went about a mile before he ordered me to make a right onto a small dead-end street. It was lined with undeveloped land and a few isolated homes. There were no street lamps, only the car's headlights, as darkness sucked us in.

"Is this where you dumped Nicola's body?" I asked him.

He spread his lips into a sneer.

"Mind if I smoke?" I asked.

"A last cigarette?" He cackled.

"Yeah. I gave them up awhile back. But now I don't have to worry about my health anymore."

He threw his head back to howl. Then he reached into his shirt pocket and offered me a Marlboro. I took one and pushed in the dashboard lighter.

"Tell me something, Pike." I said.

"Yeah?"

"Did you off Nicola and Chloe?"

I heard him snicker.

I faced him. "Do you know who did?"

He laughed some more. Like he was in on some private joke.

The cigarette lighter popped. I took it out and lit my cigarette.

That was my cue.

In a flash, I flung the hot lighter into the top of his open shirt as I stomped on the brakes.

He cried out as I pushed the gun out of my way. It discharged and I felt the bullet pass across my ribs and stomach. I gripped his hand and rammed it against the dashboard, again and again. The pistol went off several times, *pop—pop*, hitting the windshield. The shattered glass showered down on us.

His other hand was busy trying to retrieve the lighter that was burning his skin. I smelled his polyester shirt as it melted onto him.

He dropped the gun.

I scooped it up and took aim. He already had the door open. Both hands tearing his shirt open. I pulled the trigger. The bullet ripped into his back as he rushed out of the door. He fell onto one knee, recovered, and got to his feet again. He headed toward the small launching dock at the end of the road, his body glowing in the beams of the headlights.

I got out of the car and hurried after him. I found him at the wooden wharf. He was on his stomach, a bloodstain spreading across the back of his shirt.

"PIKE!"

He turned onto his side and tried to stand up. But it was no use. His legs were wet noodles. He glared up at me. He was out of breath. In pain. His snaky smile long gone.

I held the Browning out in front of me. Now I was smiling. "Is this where you dumped Nicola's body?"

He cringed when he shifted position.

"This is where it ends for you, Pike." I declared.

He showed his teeth—the best he could muster up for a smile.

"You know who killed them." I persisted.

Silence. Just an all-knowing expression on his face.

"Isn't that right, Pike?"

He nodded.

"You stole the tape with Nicola and me on it— didn't you?

"Pretty hot stuff." He grinned perversely.

"Did you catch the end . . . the part when the murderer enters the picture?"

"Never did get that far . . ."

"No, you wouldn't. Too busy getting off on the action. Who did it, Pike? If it wasn't you, who was it?"

He broke into a full, nasty smile. "You'll find out soon enough."

"TELL ME!" I shouted, my words bouncing back at me in a ricocheting echo.

He shook his head. "Talk about your lifetime memberships." He snickered.

I knew I wasn't going to get anything out of this asshole. I aimed the pistol at him—dead center of his forehead. "I just cancelled your lifetime membership, Pike."

And then I squeezed the trigger.

In that instant, I flashed on my confrontation with the Dagger Intruder in that Lower East Side tenement apartment. I held him at bay with my weapon as he finished dressing. The woman remained on the floor, her body heaving.

"Who are you?" Thomas asked again.

I waved my gun to direct him out of the room. He slunk along the wall as he inched his way out to the kitchen.

Holding my gun on him, I crouched down to assist his victim. I pushed down her nightgown to cover her bruised nakedness. Then I removed her gag. She let out a loud sob as I helped her to her feet. I picked up Thomas's weapon—a thin double-edged dagger—and pocketed it.

He stood in the doorway, his hands raised in the air.

As soon as the woman regained her bearings, she launched at her attacker. Her fingernails were in his face, leaving a trail of torn flesh behind. I seized her and pulled her away, her legs kicking in defiance.

Thomas bolted. The woman lashed out against me. I brought my pistol down on the top of her head with one brisk movement that disabled her. She collapsed to the floor like a rag doll.

I started after him. I reached the window just as he stepped out onto the fire escape. I grabbed hold of his leg and yanked, making him fall on his face. I pulled myself onto the fire escape and apprehended him, my gun pressed against the base of his skull. "FREEZE!"

He stopped resisting, his chest heaving as he tried to catch his breath.

"Now, let's be a good boy and get on your feet—carefully!"

He slowly stood up, my gun against his head. I pushed him through the window and threw him to the floor. He sat there, his forehead beaded with sweat.

"Who the fuck are you, man?" He asked.

I sat on the edge of the cocktail table and aimed my gun in his face. "I want to know if you ever used an ice pick during one of your dirty numbers?"

He eyed me confoundedly.

"Did you?"

He was about to shake his head when I whipped my pistol across his face sending a shower of teeth and blood airborne. He held his jaw, his head reeling from the impact.

"ANSWER ME!" I demanded.

"NO!" He sprayed back, a bloody gap where his front teeth used to be.

"THE TRUTH!"

"Did you ever stick one of your victims?" I continued my interrogation. "Did you ever work the Upper East Side?"

His head rocked back and forth, his heavy eyelids half-drawn over his eyeballs. He was fading fast.

I straightened up and pushed him onto his back with my foot. He stared up at me with dreamy liquid eyes.

I brought my knee up and stomped down hard on his crotch. He let out a shriek as I grounded his balls into the floor.

That revitalized him.

I placed my foot on his chest and peered down at him. Tears streamed down his face. He managed to get out, "You mutherfucker!"

I guffawed.

Sobering up, I asked: "Did you ever stick a white lady? Huh? Or do you only have the hots for spicks?"

"I'd fuck your mother, you piece of—"

I applied pressure to his chest with my foot that made him clam up.

"Only answer the question!"

"I ain't saying shit without my lawyer!" He proclaimed.

"You ain't gettin' it, pal. I'm not the fuckin' law, you asshole!" I shouted. "I'm here to take your head off!"

"You're goin' to be in a shitload of trouble, man." He threatened.

"Maybe." I sang. "Maybe. But at least I'll still be breathin', y'know what I mean?" I grinned.

"You're fuckin' crazy!" He began to squirm beneath my foot.

"All I want from you are some answers. Then I'll let you go."

"Yeah, right." He wasn't buying it.

"Did you ever work uptown?" I asked again.

"Maybe." He retorted.

"The Upper East Side?"

"Probably."

"Did you ever use an ice pick?"

"No."

"What about the ice pick you used on your old man?"

"How do you know about that?" He asked.

"Come on, pal, let's just cut through the crap and get right to it. Did you stick an ice pick in Kate Mitchum's ear last October in her Upper East Side apartment?"

"No fuckin' way!" He replied, blood spraying from his mouth.

"How come it follows the same patterns of your other crimes? The break-in and entering, the assault with a weapon—everything but the rape. What happened? She kick you in the balls? What made you stick her, you slimy scumbag?" I sneered.

He stared up at me silently. His face and clothes bloody from my attack.

"ANSWER ME!"

"Get stuffed!" He shot back.

When I looked up, I saw the Hispanic woman standing in the doorway. Blood trickled down her face from her head wound. She stood there in a daze. She was about forty, a little plump, her dark hair speckled with gray.

"Call the police." I told her.

She hesitated.

"NOW!" I insisted.

She turned and wandered into the kitchen where the phone was mounted on the wall.

As I watched her, I felt a motion beneath me. It was Thomas. He was making a grab for my gun.

I put all my weight on his chest, literally standing on him.

He seized my foot and tried to push it off of him.

"Move and I'll blow you away!" I said.

He ignored my threats.

I waved my gun in his face to remind him.

He grabbed hold of the pistol with both his hands and squeezed. The gun discharged, sending a bullet into floor. I heard the woman scream in the background as we continued to struggle. He was counting on me being too chickenshit to pull the trigger.

How wrong he was.

I managed to get away from him. I backed away as he sat up. Something snapped inside my head. The pressure was mounting after all these months of tracking this animal down. I felt the steam escaping as I advanced towards him. . . .

"Okay, if you want it, here it is!" I said as I shoved the gun into his mouth and pulled the trigger.

Realizing what I had just done, I collapsed onto my knees. A numbness spread from my hand, all the way up my arm, and throughout my body. There was a ringing in my ear. Deafening. As though the sound of the gunshot was trapped inside my head.

The woman came running in, paused at the doorway, and screamed at the sight of the bloody corpse below me. She ran across the kitchen and out the front door, her arms flailing, her screeching lungs at full volume.

Automatically I reached into the pocket of my leather bomber jacket and took out his dagger. I placed it in his hand. I would need a story for the police.

I would plead self-defense.

I went to the sofa and plopped down on it in a stupor. The ringing continued . . . the numbness now working on my brain. I remained there until the police arrived. The stench of death invading my nostrils.

Later the police took me down to the precinct. After preliminary questioning from a few local detectives, Internal Affairs decided to stick their nose into the case and sent over the notorious Romanus.

I was sitting alone in a interrogation room when the crater-faced Romanus entered. He was wearing a brown Sears-Roebuck wash and wear suit, a pink shirt, and a pin-dot pattern polyester tie. Right away from the way he dressed, I hated this man's guts.

"Mitchum." He said with a nod then sat down adjacent from me.

"What brings Internal Affairs into the picture—I'm an *ex*-cop?" I sighed.

"Seems to be more to this than you're letting on." He clucked his tongue as he read my statement. "Let me get this straight. You were out for a walk when you suddenly saw the perpetrator climb up the fire escape of a tenement building and break-in to an apartment?" He eyed me in disbelief. "What the fuck were you doing walking around that neighborhood in the middle of the night?"

I shrugged. "Gettin' some air."

He nodded with a grin. "Very amusing, Mitchum. I just want to know how you found out about Thomas— who leaked it to you?" He lit up a cigarette.

"I read about him in the papers." I replied.

"We didn't leak the story to the papers. We kept it under wraps so we could conduct a surveillance on this suspect." He related, the cigarette dangling from his lips.

"A surveillance?" I couldn't restrain the surprised tone in my voice.

"Yes," he smirked, "we were watching you watching him."

I sat back in my chair and tossed him a cold eye. "Is that a fact?"

"Yes." He was very pleased with himself. "You were seen meeting with one of our detectives . . . Matrix."

"Just chewed some fat . . . old cops and robbers stories." I tried to make it sound as frivolous as I could but I knew he had me.

"Really?" He exhaled a stream of smoke from his nostrils like a fiery dragon. "Funny, that's not what Matrix told me."

"He's just a kid . . . with a wild imagination. Maybe I told him too many old wives' tales." I chuckled.

"He gave you departmental data." Romanus stated in a flat monotone.

"Leave the kid out of this."

"I'm afraid I can't." Romanus stamped out his cigarette. "He's just been suspended awaiting a hear-

ing.'' Then with a twinkle in his eye he added,
''Without pay.''

''You son-of-a-bitch.'' I uttered.

''Them the breaks, cowboy.'' Romanus flashed
his teeth. ''It was one thing to blow Thomas away.
Sure, it might've been self-defense but I seriously
doubt it. Not with your Gestapo-like tactics. No cop I
ever heard of shoves his pistol down a suspect's
throat and pulls the trigger in self-defense. That's
precious. There's not much I can do about nailing
you on that one. But maybe knowing that you destroyed a young man's career will be punishment
enough. Maybe. But since you don't seem to have a
conscience, I doubt you give a shit about anything.
Isn't that right, Mitchum?''

I shot up and seized Romanus by his jacket lapels
and slapped him hard on either side of his ugly face.
Then I shoved him back into his chair. He shook his
dazed head and snapped out of it. That was when he
went for his revolver.

''HOLD IT!'' Adam shouted as he came running
into the room with another officer.

They pulled us apart.

''Alright you guys—cool down!'' Adam held me
back.

Romanus snarled at me. ''I'm going to report this—
you assaulted a police officer!''

''You call yourself a police officer? You're nothing but a fuckin' candyass!'' I sneered back at him.

Adam walked me out of the room. He pinned me
against the wall outside in the hall. ''What in God's
name are you doin'?''

''I'm goin' to tear his lungs out!'' I threatened.

Adam shoved me around, trying to knock some sense into me. "Look at yourself, man. You're actin' like some fuckin' animal! Chill out! Haven't you caused enough damage in one day? You blow some poor dude's head off and get a good cop suspended."

I stopped resisting and slowly slid down the wall to the floor, my energy drained from me.

"I want you out of here. I don't ever want to see your face again!" Adam snapped.

"Come on, Adam." I said weakly.

"I mean it, Mitch. Do me . . . do all of us a favor and get out of the city. You're a fuckin' menace!" He walked away from me. When he turned the corner he ran into Jesse. They exchanged a few words. Then she approached me with apprehension. Her eyes welled up with tears.

I remained sitting on the cold floor.

She glanced down at me, her lower jaw quivering. "Mitch . . ."

I covered my face with my hands. I just wanted to coil up and disappear from the face of the earth.

It was then that I had decided to take everybody's advice, and leave the city. To go to the Hamptons. *The Promised Land.*

But eventually everything catches up with you. . . .

26

PROMISED LAND

SAM RAYBURN had been one of the earlier film school graduates to make it in Hollywood. He had paved the way for the other "Hollywood Brats" to follow. Starting out as a screenwriter, he had won an Oscar for his very first produced screenplay. He went on to become one of the most powerful directors in the United States. The man with the Midas Touch. His films were considered artistic and commercial. Transcending genres, like westerns and gangster pics, he created post-modernistic masterpieces. He tried to run his own studio and produce his colleagues' projects. But since he didn't have proper financial support the studio had foundered. That was the start of his downfall in Hollywood.

Then came his war epic about Central America, *Casualties*. He had wanted to shoot a fictional, anti-war film against the background of an actual military conflict. It had sounded great. It also sounded dangerous. But the challenge urged him on. He had written a poignant and controversial screenplay, then put together a super cast and crew. Only the cream of the crop.

But as soon as filming had begun, the trouble started. Death threats from both government and leftist guerrillas were only the tip of the iceberg. Disease had swept through the cast and crew. There were complaints of poor working conditions. As the picture fell behind schedule, millions of dollars continued to be spent. The studio executives were getting worried. There had been talk of pulling the plug.

And then the worst thing imaginable had occurred....

It was a simple, standard special effect. An exploding grenade. The F/X team had set things up. The star, Jack Quinn, and leading actress, Amy Robertson, were to run through some jungle terrain away from hostile guerrillas. A grenade was to be thrown by Quinn. The camera was stationed in front of them. The telephoto lens would capture them as they dashed through the jungle toward the camera. Just when he reached his mark before the camera, Quinn would turn, pull the pin, and toss the grenade at the guerrillas. The grenade was a fake. It was empty. The ground where he was to throw it was rigged to explode.

Rayburn, dressed in Army fatigues and a stained green athletic undershirt, was crouched beneath the camera. He had a full beard. He was pale and gaunt. His brown eyes hidden behind a tense brow. He would talk the actors through the scene like a silent movie director. Later the sound would be dubbed in.

At the cry of "ACTION!", the actors began their gauntlet. Robertson gripped Quinn's arm as they ran toward the camera and crew. Rayburn was shouting, his whole body animated. He shot up and urged them on. "MORE EMOTION!" He screamed out. "SHOW FEAR!" He continued.

They were halfway there when it happened.

The explosion erupted beneath their feet. Their bodies were thrown to the sky as dirt and smoke enveloped the area. Rayburn raced to them. Before he could reach them, another explosion tore up the path. Rayburn was thrown backwards, debris showering all around him.

When the smoke cleared there were two dead and several wounded. Including Rayburn. He would later lose his left eye.

The media had had a field day with the tragedy. Two Hollywood superstars had been killed on a movie location. No one knew what had gone wrong. The production company had charged sabotage. The government had blamed the leftist guerrillas; Rayburn his F/X crew. They had all blamed him. And round-and-round it went. Lawsuits had been filed. Rayburn had turned out to be the loser. He was railroaded out of Hollywood. After buying a house in a secluded area of the Hamptons, his wife and two children soon left him.

He lived alone in a huge house in an area known as the Promised Land. It had gotten its name many years ago when Congress set aside land on the beach for fish factories. But the factories were all in ruins now. I had heard rumors that Rayburn converted an old factory into a post-production studio. He was cutting *Casualties* there. All alone with his unfinished epic. It sounded pretty pathetic.

I drove Pike's Buick out to Rayburn's place. His house was on Cranberry Hole Road. It wasn't easy to find in the darkness. The house was set off from the road. A big gray driftwood number with numerous windows and solar panels on the roof. An old fish factory was a few yards to the right of it. A high chain link fence with barbed wire surrounded it. I drove up the illuminated driveway. There was a jeep parked in front of me. It didn't seem to belong there standing before such a luxurious house. I got out and headed for the door.

That was when I heard the growl behind me. I swung around and saw the blue-black Doberman pinscher staring up at me with dead shark-like eyes. His dagger teeth glistened in the darkness. A good two-feet high at the shoulders, the animal wore a black and silver studded collar. His loud bark sent shivers through my body.

I slowly moved my hand toward my pistol tucked in the waistband of my jeans. I halted when the dog stepped forward. "Okay, boy, cool it." I said softly, my voice cracking from nervousness.

I heard rattling keys in the direction of the gate outside the fish factory. I was afraid to look, to move a single muscle, to even breath. Our eyes were locked. Gleaming saliva drooled from his menacing jaws. I heard footsteps. I held my stance as I shifted my eyes slowly to the side.

I saw a shadow of a man walking towards me out of the corner of my eye.

He came into the light and grabbed hold of the dog's collar. "Good girl." He said affectionately.

He gazed at me with his one eye. A black patch concealed the other. His gray-streaked brown mane of wild hair and beard almost made him unrecognizable. He was dressed in green fatigues and a soiled white tee-shirt. He was very lean . . . bony. His pale olive complexion made him look ill. When he spoke, his fat, rubbery lips hardly moved. "This is private property."

"Lucky you came by before I blew your pet all the way to dog heaven." I proclaimed.

He pulled back his lips and showed his crooked grin. "Ginger here would have torn a chunk out of your neck before you even laid a hand on your weapon."

"House-broken is she?"

He laughed. "And then some."

"I always wanted to meet you, Mr. Rayburn."

"You and a million others." He replied.

"Modest type, huh?" I asked sarcastically.

"You have a name?"

"Mitchum." I said with smile. "Jeff Mitchum."

"Mitchum." Rayburn tossed the name around in his head for awhile and came up dry. "Am I supposed to know you?"

"Maybe." I retorted. "I'm a friend of a friend."

"And who's the friend?"

I said, "Brandon Gage."

A smirk, then: "He isn't any friend of mine."

"I can understand that. But he does work for you."

"Something like that . . . trouble is, Gage doesn't like to work for anybody."

"I think we're on the same wavelength, Mr. Rayburn." I implied.

"So what brings you here?"

"Gage and RayBeam."

"Go on."

I took my time to add, "And murder."

Rayburn got serious again. "Murder?"

"We have to talk, Rayburn."

He looked me in the eye and said, "Sure sounds like it."

27

VIDEO MESSIAH

I FOLLOWED RAYBURN through the locked gate and into the factory. The weathered building was in need of fresh paint and repair. But inside was a high-tech work studio. Before us stood a bank of sixteen video monitors, stacked four-by-four. Our images as well as those of the interior and exterior of the house and grounds were displayed.

I whistled in admiration.

It was like walking into a fun house of mirrors.

A soft-cushioned chair with remote controls was positioned before the monitors.

"A little touch of Orwell in the night?" I asked.

Rayburn had to turn his head to look at me. He shrugged. "My eyesight has been hindered. These," he raised his arms, "are now my eyes."

I remembered reading about Rayburn's interest in video technology. He felt all our entertainment would be produced through electronic means someday. Toward the end of his Hollywood career, he had become increasingly obsessed with new technology. Critics felt he was more concerned with hardware than software. That he had lost his heart somewhere along the way. Now I saw how far he had come.

"You work here alone?"

"Yes . . . I spend most of my time here. I have editing equipment in the back. I've been cutting some footage." He informed me.

"*Casualties*?"

"Ironic title—don't you think?" He faced me again, his brown eye burning into me. Then he grinned again. "Have you seen any of my work?"

"Sure. I think you were . . . I mean, are the best."

He laughed at my blunder. "Don't worry . . . Hollywood already has me dead and buried."

"But you're still a young man."

He nodded. "True. But film is dead. It died with my old life."

"What's next—video?" I inquired.

"And beyond. Before long, I'll be able to shoot an entire film right here in this converted factory. It could be set anywhere in the world. With the digital process I could create backdrops that will rival only the real thing. Shoot two actors against that wall, add the background later."

"Pretty remarkable." I can see how excited he became when he talked about it. Poor bastard probably only wanted to get back to work.

"Future technology is on my side." He said gleefully. Maybe he really believed what some fortune-teller told him. "But you came here to tell me something."

"Yes, but we need a couple more guests to join us."

"Guests?"

"Gage and his girlfriend, Zoe Savage."

He cocked his head like a bird to take me in. "I don't understand."

"I'll explain it all to you, but first I want you to make a call to Gage. Have him come over here. Tell him that I'm here."

He sat down on the chair and opened a door built into the arm. He pulled out a cordless telephone and punched in the number. A few moments later he said, "Gage? This is Sam. I have a young man here who says he's a friend of yours. That's right. His name is Mitchum. Y'know him? Something wrong, Gage? Okay, come by the factory. Oh, and bring Zoe along. You never told me about her, Gage. Uh-huh. Sure, I understand. See you in a couple." He hung up and swung around in the chair to face me. He was beaming. "Gage doesn't sound too happy."

"Can't understand why." I chuckled.

"I bet." He stood up. "Come with me."

We went around the video monitors where he unlocked a steel door. We went inside a large room filled with post-production film equipment. Editing consoles. Sound dubbing gizmos. And even more monitors. It looked like a set from one of those Fifties' science-fiction movies—only slicker. We sat down on stools before a work table. Four thirteen-inch monitors were built into the wall.

"We can watch everything from here."

I eyed him. He looked like he was having a good

time. I noticed there was a video camera aimed at us. "Will they be able to see us?"

"If I want them to."

He played around with some knobs and a battle scene appeared on all four screens. It was the doomed footage from *Casualties*. Quinn and Robertson were sprinting through the jungle. Then the camera shook and smoke filled the screen. I could make out running figures. The camera must have fallen to the ground on its' side. I saw the back of a man darting to the scene. Rayburn? Then another explosion. The man being thrown off his feet. More smoke. The film ran out. Cut to the beginning of the shot again. Rayburn switched it off.

He must've looped it. The same scene played over and over again. Maybe he was truly insane. He didn't say anything, perhaps expecting a response from me.

Finally after a long period of dead air, he said, "I thought about working around it. Rewriting it. Killing the protagonists off half-way through the picture isn't revolutionary. Hitchcock pulled that off in *Psycho*. I might be able to do something with the footage I shot. Shoot the rest of it here. Electronically fill in the background. Y'know what I mean?"

I nodded.

"Know much about film?"

"Some. I run a video rental store in East Hampton."

"Really?"

"Yep."

"I send one of my servants out to your shop to buy something every once in awhile. I have a good library all my own. Show it to you some time."

I cleared my throat. I thought it was time to get down to business. "About Gage."

"Yes?"

"I have a lot to tell."

He eyed me. "I'm all ears."

We watched them on the monitors as Savage's car pulled up behind Pike's Buick. Gage was behind the wheel. He shut off the engine. Then they looked at one another. Their lips moving. Savage opened the door and stepped out in the misty air.

That was when Ginger came trotting toward her.

Rayburn swiftly grabbed the microphone and snapped, "Heel, Ginger."

The animal halted in her tracks.

Gage gazed across the roof of the auto at Savage.

Rayburn's voice boomed over the loudspeaker, "Come into the factory, Brandon."

Gage shut the door and walked around the car to join his mistress. She wrapped her arm around his.

I addressed Rayburn. "Has Gage ever been inside the factory before?"

Rayburn shook his head. "Only the house."

"That's good."

The couple came through the gate and went inside the factory. Rayburn's closed-circuit cameras followed their every move. They were staring up at the bank of monitors.

"I feel like the Wizard of Oz." Rayburn joked. He switched on the camera so that they could view us.

I waved.

"Good evening, Brandon . . . Ms. Savage." Rayburn said.

"What's this all about?" Gage asked, still dressed in his whites.

"That's what I would like to know." Rayburn replied.

"It's all about your scam, Gage." I said. "Your pal, Pike, he didn't make it. He's got a third eye smack in the middle of his forehead. He never did have much luck with me."

Gage turned as white as his clothes. He swallowed hard and eyed Savage.

"I filled Mr. Rayburn in on your little scheme to take over RayBeam. He didn't seem too surprised by it. But he didn't like the bit about offing your wife and kid."

"I HAD NOTHING TO DO WITH THAT!" He shouted at the video screens.

"Well, somebody did, Gage." I said. "Isn't that right, Zoe?"

Gage whipped his head to look at her. "What's he talking about?"

"He's jerking us off, Brandon."

"Somebody's jerking off somebody—that's for sure." I added.

"You're the one who's wanted by the police." Gage said.

"Not anymore. A woman with long dark hair was seen at both murders."

"Long dark hair?" Gage repeated to himself. He tossed it around for awhile.

"Don't you see what he's trying to do?" Savage said.

"Obviously murder isn't beneath you, Gage. You didn't even flinch when Pike blew Janet's brains out. You ordered him to take care of me. Why not waste your family if they're not included in your plans?"

"I wouldn't do that." Gage shook his head. "Not to my Chloe."

"Ohhh . . . is that remorse I hear in your voice?"

"Listen you . . . none of this messy business would've come about if it wasn't for your goddamn interference!"

"My interference?" I laughed. "You tried to hang a few murder raps on me."

"I swear to God, I didn't have anything to do with those killings!" Gage insisted.

"Then why did you have Pike dispose of your wife's body?"

"What choice did I have? I was in the middle of an illegal operation. If I called in the police it would've brought attention to me. Believe me, I wasn't behind it. If I wanted to split from my wife, I would've divorced her."

"Maybe she turned you down. Maybe you had no choice . . ." I pursued the matter.

He shook his head. "NO! I never even asked her for one."

"BRANDON!" Savage screeched.

"She was my wife, dammit!" Gage shouted back at her. He turned away from her and walked to the other side of the room.

"You told me you had asked for a divorce . . . that she wouldn't give you one. That she would take you for every last dime you had."

He kept his back to her, dropping his head in defeat.

"You said you were going to marry me." She continued as tears filled her eyes.

I covered the mike. "Are you recording this?"

Rayburn nodded enthusiastically. "It's going to be great."

"I'm sorry, Zoe." Gage said. "Can't you see—it's over. We're finished. They know everything."

"Everything but who killed your family." I said. "A woman with long dark hair. She wore a yellow slicker and sunglasses. She used an ice pick. Know anybody who fits that description, Gage? Know somebody who might have a reason to murder them? To clear the way, perhaps?"

He turned slowly around to face Savage. He looked at her for awhile in silence. She clutched her handbag with both hands to her breasts. Her face streaked with black mascara and tears. She shook her head. "I DIDN'T DO IT!"

He ran his hand through his hair. "I had no idea you were capable of such a thing . . ."

"YOU CAN'T THINK THAT I DID IT!" She screamed angrily.

He gazed up at the monitors. His cold eyes were now welled up with tears. "I had no idea . . ." He repeated in a stupor.

"YOU'RE NOT GOING TO PIN THIS ON ME!" She shouted at him. "YOU BASTARD!!" She reached into her handbag and pulled out a stainless steel Bauer .22 automatic pistol. The bag fell to her feet as she held the small weapon in her two hands.

Gage put his hands up. "Zoe . . ."

She pulled the trigger again and again, and emptied the five bullets into him.

Gage took each shot standing there in disbelief. His face showed no trace of pain. His arms wrapped around himself. He opened his mouth but no words came out . . . only a small trickle of blood. His knees buckled and he collapsed onto the concrete floor.

She beheld the smoking weapon with disgust and threw it at the monitors. ''YOU'RE ALL BASTARDS!''

She ran out of the building.

I stood up to go after her but Rayburn put his hand on my shoulder and eased me back onto the stool. ''Ginger will take care of her.''

''You can't be serious, Rayburn.'' I shot up again and glanced at the monitors. But it was already too late. The dog was on her. The powerful jaws at her throat. Her screams poured out of the speakers.

I bolted out of the building with the Browning in hand. When I got to the scene, Ginger was dragging the limp body away. I raised my weapon and squeezed the trigger three consecutive times. The dog let out a painful yelp and staggered for a few moments before succumbing to death.

I stood there in the cool misty air, the gun at my side. The dog lay at Savage's feet. Blood drained from the large tear at her neck. Her eyes were open. Her white blouse torn and bloodied.

Then headlights fell on me from behind. I turned around and watched Montana's limo pull up. The chauffeur opened the rear door and held an umbrella for his lord and master. Montana, wrapped in a khaki trench coat, walked over to me. He took in Savage's body. Then he faced me. "Gage?"

"Inside. Dead. Her." I said, my voice drained of emotion.

"Good." Montana replied.

Rayburn came out to join us. "You didn't have to do that, Mitchum."

"You could've stopped it." I remarked.

"It makes it easier for us this way." Rayburn said.

"You have it captured on tape?" Montana asked.

"All of it." Rayburn retorted gleefully.

"Well, that clears you, Mitchum." Montana said.

I stepped back away from them so I could get a better look at them. "You two were in on this from the start?"

"I got a tip from a valuable source about Gage's plans to buy the company out from under me. I didn't know how to handle it . . . how to prove it. I asked Montana for advice." Rayburn explained.

"You two buddies?" I asked sarcastically.

"We go back a few." Rayburn smirked.

I shook my head. "Real nice people."

"I said I would take care of you, Mitchum." Montana mentioned sincerely.

"I don't want anything from you . . . any of you!" I said through clenched teeth and walked away.

epilogue

A LIFETIME MEMBERSHIP

AFTER A WHILE, the bad dreams had subsided. It was as though reliving the ordeal had exorcised the demons once and for all. I had a lot of guilt to unload. Especially about Matrix. I had tried to make amends with him shortly after I heard he was suspended from the force. But he had refused to see me. He wouldn't even return my calls. Zip. The next thing I heard, the day before his hearing was scheduled, Adam called to tell me that Matrix had swallowed a bottle of Quaaludes.

That's when I had decided to go into business for myself and run a video store. I was always a movie buff, so I thought it would be natural for me to get into video. Besides, I thought it would help me keep my mind off of all that had transpired. Movies were an escape for me. Unfortunately, the brain is like a video camera . . . it records memories. The good and especially the bad. I could never lose the images. . . .

They had never found Nicola's body. They had searched the area where Pike had taken me. Even underwater. But to this day they have never recovered her body.

Montana had kept his promise and restored my shop, also making me keep the Porsche. It had taken me a while to deal with it but I figured what the hell, I had earned it.

The police had the videotape as evidence that Gage and Savage were guilty. I had been acquitted of any murder charges against me including Pike's death by reason of self-defense.

The media blitz that had followed brought a great deal of renewed interest to Rayburn. He had been interviewed by the national weeklies and the major television broadcasters. He was back in the limelight again, signing numerous film deals, including one to finish his opus, *Casualties*.

Adam had stayed angry with me for a short time after. But we've since kissed and made up. I had even invited him and his wife to the wedding.

Yeah, I had done it. Again. It had been about the only thing I could do to make it up to Jesse. She had gone through the wringer for me. Besides, there had been another good reason. . . .

So I thought my life was back on track again until that gray, bleak April morning. It was one of those days when I should've stayed in bed. It was wet and muggy outside. Again, we had gone directly from winter into summer without much of a spring. I was down in the basement doing the laundry. Jesse was up in the media room listening to the stereo. I was transferring the wet clothes from the washer to the dryer when I realized I was all out of cling-free pads. So I went to the back wall where we stored our supplies. I always kept a hefty stock of things. Going through the shelves I found it.

My heart skipped a beat.

There tucked behind the Brillo pads and Tide, was a rolled up yellow slicker. Wrapped inside was a pair of Porsche Design sunglasses and a black-haired wig.

I stood there awhile feeling my heart pounding in my chest. Thoughts raced through my mind. Had somebody planted these? Was this somebody's idea of a sick joke? But no matter how many ways I thought around it, I always came back to one thing.

The ice pick.

It had always nagged at me that the weapon used on Nicola and Chloe had been an ice pick. Had somebody been fucking with my mind? Had someone intentionally copied my former wife's murder?

Or did the same person who had killed Kate also murder the others? It was too coincidental to be anything else. And only one person had been there all the time. One very jealous woman. It had never even crossed my mind. I just couldn't believe it. Didn't want to believe it.

I rolled up the evidence and dropped it into an empty carton. Why had she kept this incriminating stuff around—did she plan on using it again? I would have to dispose of it later.

In a trance, I went slowly up the stairs to the top landing. I heard Eric Clapton singing "Forever Man" on the stereo.

I opened the door that led into the dining room. I turned the corner and entered the media room. I stood there in the doorway watching her.

She was plopped on the leather sofa. She was knitting. The pink and blue yarns were at her side. She was working the long pointy needles carefully on the little booties. Her arms resting on her bulging belly.

It had happened *that* night. The night before my whole life had changed. The night before Pike had walked into the shop. Before Nicola. And Chloe. That drunken night when I had promised Jesse something that had escaped my mind.

Until now.

Now I remembered. As Eric Clapton strummed on his electric guitar, it all came back to me. That night. I had promised to be her forever man. Or else.

She had told me about Kate that night. How Kate had made her jealous when she tried to remain friendly with me. That she never wanted to feel that way ever again.

And I had promised her.

It would never happen again.

Then the very next day, Nicola had come into my shop. Jesse must have been watching me . . . testing me.

I guess I had failed the test.

She looked up from her knitting and gave me her crooked grin. I gazed at her swelled belly that held eight months of child inside. Our love child.

Now I knew the true meaning of a lifetime membership.

CRITIC'S CHOICE

For action-packed suspense thrillers.

CRITIC'S CHOICE
The greatest mysteries being published today

CRITIC'S CHOICE

The finest in HORROR and OCCULT